BEAUTY & HER BEASTLY LOVE

Rosetta Bloom

ISBN: 1519631936
ISBN-13: 978-1519631930

ABOUT THIS SERIES

Many of our favorite fairy tales from childhood, such as *The Princess and the Pea*, *Beauty and the Beast*, and *Cinderella*, originated centuries ago. Over the years, they've been told and retold by different authors in different media, each retelling adding its own spin. Here, we take these classic tales and give them a spin that is full-on sexy. While these tales are not the bedtime stories you would ever read to a child, they are definitely meant to be enjoyed in bed. These retellings preserve the base of the story, but add new twists and include passion, lust, and the fulfillment of carnal desires. I hope you enjoy them.

May your love always be in bloom.

-Rosetta.

CONTENTS

1

Beauty ran her finger over the imprint of the rose on the leather-bound book, savoring the supple feel of it beneath her fingertips. It was smooth and firm, yet soft enough that it felt almost like skin. She wondered briefly if it felt like the skin of a man's erection. The type of man she'd read about in this book. In the other books like it.

She smiled to herself, her red lips curving delightedly as she thought about what she'd just read in this book's pages. The man and woman in their bedroom, the passion with which he'd removed her clothing: speedy, furious, ripping, tearing, beastly. The moans of pleasure that escaped her as he took her. Their bodies naked, groping, clinging to each other.

Beauty wondered if these books were true. Yes, she knew that men and women bedded each other, but the passion with which the people in these books acted and reacted seemed unreal. Were there really people out there that loved each other so fully, that reacted so primally, fiercely and all-consumingly? Did people really do those things? Did they really touch each other like that? The warmth between her legs hinted that it was very real indeed, but she didn't know for sure. She might never know. Beauty was rarely allowed around others. She lived in the country with her father, Pierre LaVigne. He was a kind man who made his living farming. He grew grapes and made wine, but, ironically, he lacked spirit.

He was a man broken by loss. The loss of her mother, Celine. Renowned for her beauty and horticultural skills, her mother had taken ill suddenly and died when Beauty was just six years old. Pierre had persevered, and her older twin brothers, Marcel and Maurice, had pitched in to help. The vineyard had run smoothly until Beauty turned 12. Until then, Beauty had been able to walk the two miles to

1

town and attend school or visit the shops at the market. Then Marcel and Maurice had become ill working in the fields. They died within a day of each other. It was so sudden, so quick, that Pierre was in shock. He could do almost nothing.

Nothing but pull in the reigns. He farmed less land, grew fewer grapes, made less wine, and demanded that Beauty stay at the homestead only. He allowed her to help press the wine, but never to work in the fields the way her brothers had. She milked the cow, tended the vegetable and flower gardens and sometimes read over the gardening journals her mother had left.

Often she read. Her father indulged her love of books, letting a local shopkeeper, Giselle, bring her books from Giselle's personal library. Giselle was also supposed to answer feminine questions that Pierre, as a man, would have no clue how to answer. Beauty loved Giselle's visits and all the books she brought. When Beauty was younger, she offered to read to her father or asked him to read to her, but he wasn't a man who enjoyed whimsical books like she did. He enjoyed the farmer's almanac and sometimes books on hunting, but nothing like the fantastical things Beauty enjoyed reading. In the last year, Beauty had been glad of her father's disinterest in her books. He rarely looked at the books Giselle brought.

About a year ago, right after Beauty had turned 17, Giselle had looked Beauty in the eyes and handed her a leather-bound book with the imprint of a Rose on it. It had no real title, in terms of what one thought of as a traditional title. It simply said "Volume I" at the top. In the center of the cover was the imprint of a rose pressed deep within the leather, and at the bottom, in seductive script, was the author's name: Ferus Lucunditas.

The old woman, her graying brown hair wrapped neatly in a scarf to keep out the oncoming winter chill, whispered to the girl: "These are special books." Giselle's dark brown eyes glanced around the room, as if she expected Beauty's father to come in from the fields and chastise them. "This is the first volume, and it discusses things women should know, things you ordinarily might learn only when you are in your husband's home. But, your life is so sheltered here, I worry that your father will not ensure your betrothal, or that you will fall into a pattern of contentment here, that you won't push to leave him. Read this so that you may learn there is more out there."

Beauty had looked down at the book, the curiosity Giselle seeded already beginning to grow. *More.* Giselle had called it more. Yes, there was more to the world than this quaint vineyard outside of town. There were bakers, shoemakers, blacksmiths, artisans, bookkeepers. There were families with husbands, wives, and gaggles of children. Beauty knew all these things, but the way that Giselle had said "more," she'd known it meant something else, something that was so much more.

She'd known instinctively by Giselle's demeanor and words that she should not read the book around her father. Even though he never expressed much interest in her books, she knew this one should be kept from him, that it would not be right to even read the book in the same room with him.

She was so glad that she had trusted her instincts. The night she'd read that first volume, she had been so shocked she gasped. Then she read it again, because she liked it. She read it a third time and touched herself, her fingers getting slick as she tried to create the sensations that had been described so vividly on the pages. She could almost feel the young man from the volume caressing her breasts, the way he'd caressed the heroine's, sliding his fingers slowly, softly down her abdomen until he reached the tuft of wild hair that shrouded her womanhood. The thought made her shiver with desire.

The door to the house banged open, and Beauty sat up straighter, lifted the book from her lap and tucked it into her sewing basket, just as her father entered the room.

"Beauty," he said, pronouncing her nickname with warmth. Though her given name was Angelina, everyone had called the girl Beauty since she was old enough to walk. "Are you alright, dear? You look flush." He turned and looked at the roaring fireplace, then at the windows, which were shuttered for the winter. "Are you too hot?"

Beauty shook her head at her father. Pierre was a stout man, with white hair atop his head and a matching beard. Some of the school children thought he looked like St. Nicholas, but Beauty simply laughed at the notion. Her father was a kind man, who happened to look older than his years because he was so marred by experience.

"I'm well, Papa," she said. "Don't worry about me."

He sighed. "Sometimes, I think that's all I do, Beauty." He took off his coat and hung it on a hook near the fireplace in their cottage. The front door opened into the main room. The house also included a kitchen and two tiny bedrooms. One for Beauty and one for her father. Had Beauty's mother, Celine, lived, there might have been more children. But they all had died: Celine, Maurice and Marcel. Now, it was just Beauty and Pierre.

Beauty stood and walked to the corner, where a jug of cider sat. "Father, would you like me to warm you a mug?" she asked as she picked up the jug and a tin cup that she could warm over the fire.

Pierre shook his head. "No, my dear," he said, sighing. "Sit, sit. I have news for you."

Beauty set the jug down and walked back to the armchair she'd been sitting in when her father had entered. He sat across from her in the other armchair. Their home was modest, but these chairs, pieces her mother had brought with her from her own home, were ornate and plush, even after all these years.

"What is the news, Papa?"

He looked down at his hands, then at Beauty. "My dear, you know your kind tutor who brings you books each week, Giselle?" Beauty nodded. "Well, for some time she has been prodding me to arrange for your marriage. She says I'm getting older and if these things aren't done, and something were to happen to me, you would be destitute, and no telling what would happen."

Beauty nodded. Giselle had told Beauty much the same. And she had given her the books. So, Beauty had yearned for her own reasons to be wed. She tried not to smile at the thoughts of what that would mean, at the pleasure of what she would experience upon being wed, assuming she were wed to a kind man, like the ones in the books. "You've found a match?"

"I think," he said. "I need to set off tomorrow to finalize the deal. The young man's family is a day's ride from here. His father sent word he'd like to make the arrangements tomorrow, before winter takes hold too strongly. And then in spring, when the thaw comes, you will be married."

Beauty offered an appropriate smile. "Papa, I thank you for your hard work on this," she said. "Might I inquire more about my husband, briefly?"

He smiled kindly, for he always seemed to appreciate Beauty's inquisitiveness. "Of course, Beauty."

"Is he kind?" she asked, for that was the only thing that mattered. She didn't care if he were handsome, as that faded over time. Her father was the perfect example. He was supposedly quite a catch in his day. His looks were gone, as were a few of his teeth, but his kindness remained. She imagined a cruel man would be forever cruel.

Pierre chuckled. "You always get to the heart of things, my dear." He pursed his lips and thought for a moment. "From the accounts of many in town, he is a prosperous young lad who hopes to inherit his father's business as a lumber man. No one has told me they have seen him being cruel, so I can only assume he is a kind man. I actually met the man at Giselle's shop. She is a good judge of character, so I'm sure him being with her is a good sign." He smiled and gave Beauty a reassuring pat on the hand.

Beauty nodded. Giselle was a good judge of character. Beauty's smile grew wider, as she thought briefly of the passage she had read the other day. "He was gentle and kind to all he met, but at night in the bed chamber, his kindness caused screams of pleasure to me, his mistress, as he unleashed his unbridled passion on me."

Her father chuckled again. "Beauty, you are positively delighted by this news," he said. "I am surprised. I thought maybe I was rushing you, that maybe I was mistaken, doing this too soon."

"Oh, Papa," she breathed out. "Part of me is sad at the thought of leaving you, but the other part of me does yearn, a little, to know a life in my own home, as an adult."

He reached out and patted her hand again. "You shall, my dear. Soon enough, you shall."

2

Pierre set out the next morning, the air freezing. He wondered if they should have just put off their negotiations until spring. He knew he'd get to keep his beloved daughter, the only remnant of the family he'd once had, through winter, but he hated setting off now to promise her to another. A day's ride wasn't a bad trip in the grand scheme of things, but he wished he could've found his daughter a suitor in town. Only the men in town didn't have what Pierre needed, which was money.

He had borrowed and borrowed to support their meager existence, and now it was all coming due. Too quickly, he had been told they would take his home and throw him and Beauty out on the street if he didn't settle his debts. Only, how could he settle debts in the winter when the grapes didn't grow, when he could barely make wine. Perhaps he should have had Beauty help, but he couldn't. Not after the twins had died that way. A sickness they'd caught in the fields, the doctor had said. He couldn't lose another child that way.

But, it seemed he was willing to lose a child this way. Willing to sell his daughter to pay his debts. He had met Monsieur Dumas at Giselle's shop. Giselle was a friend of Celine and had a portrait of Celine and Beauty that had been painted a few months before Celine's death. It hung in the corner of the shop, and Beauty was just six, but she still was beautiful. M. Dumas had remarked how beautiful the woman and girl were, and Pierre had said that the girl was even more beautiful now. Dumas had asked if Pierre knew the girl, and Pierre had admitted it was his daughter. Dumas said he was a lumber man from nearby and he was looking for a wife. He thought Beauty might make a good match. Pierre laughed, but M. Dumas did not. Giselle had come out with the man's book, and seemed cool to him.

When M. Dumas told Giselle of his suggestion to marry Beauty, the kind woman had simply said, "No, you need an older girl, one who can handle you better."

The man left, and Pierre had thought that would be the end of it, but it wasn't. M. Dumas came to the cottage one day. He had learned of Pierre's debts and said he could clear them all if Pierre would let him marry Beauty. Pierre had told Dumas he needed to think about it. That same day, Giselle had come by to deliver more books to Beauty and pick up the old ones. When he asked Giselle about Dumas, she admitted the rumors said he was cruel and that Pierre should not let Beauty marry him. Pierre was stunned, as Giselle almost never said a bad word about anyone.

When Dumas returned a few days later, Pierre had turned down his betrothal request. That's when Dumas had said Pierre had no choice. Beauty would become Dumas' wife, or Pierre and Beauty would spend the winter frozen in the snow. Dumas had paid all of Pierre's debts and now held the liens. If Pierre did not come sign the betrothal agreement within the next week, Dumas would foreclose on the property and put Pierre and Beauty out on the streets. But, if Pierre did sign them today, Pierre could keep Beauty until spring, and the marriage would take place then

Pierre felt guilty for lying to Beauty about her suitor. But, he knew nothing else to do. He couldn't tell her he'd promised her to an awful man so they wouldn't die in the harsh winter. He'd have to figure out something over the winter, some way to keep Beauty away from Dumas. But he needed to sign the agreement today. He was sure he could determine a better solution if he gave himself this extra time. Beauty didn't have to go anywhere until the spring. That was the saving grace, Pierre told himself as he rode down the path. His hands shook as he held the reins. It was too damn cold. He shivered as he approached the fork in the road. He would take it left, and onward to see Dumas.

And that's when it happened. Everything went white. A blizzard, seemingly from out of nowhere. He couldn't see anything, not even a few inches in front of him. He prodded the horse to go on, though it seemed it didn't want to go in any normal pattern. It trotted this way, then that, and then in a circle. Pierre didn't dare dismount though. Wherever this horse was taking him in the sea of white, he would get there quicker and more reliably on those four legs than his own two.

Pierre's face hurt with cold, his lips cracking, and his hands numb, as he tried to hold on to the horse. Finally, the wind stopped howling and the snow stopped swirling around them. He'd been out there for hours, and it was dark. The only light, from the moon, shone down on a wrought iron gate that encompassed a large manor. Pierre dismounted his horse and pushed on the gate. It opened. He guided the horse through and closed the gate. He found a stable that had stalls, fresh water, and feed. Thankful, Pierre settled his horse there, tying him to a hitching post and bringing over a bag of oats. No, it wasn't Pierre's home, but surely under the circumstance, even a true brute would understand the need to water and feed a horse after such a journey.

Pierre left the stables and wandered around to the main house. He went up to the front door and knocked. There was no answer. He knocked again, and this time the door opened a crack. "Hello," Pierre said. No response. He pushed the door open wider and went in. He saw no one. He closed the door and found himself in an entryway that was completely dark. Around the corner, he could see light emanating from another room. So, he headed toward it and was immediately struck by the warmth coming from the area. The room was a large entertaining room with a giant fireplace. There were fancy sitting chairs, a piano in the corner and two chaises. Next to one of the chairs, on an end table, was a plate filled with food. There was cheese, fruit, warm bread, hot pheasant, and a carafe of wine.

"Hello. Is anyone here?" Pierre called. No answer again. Pierre sat and ate, feeling certain the food and wine had been placed there for him. Before he knew it, he was fast asleep.

When he woke in the morning, the fire was still burning, the room was still warm, and he looked around for a sign of someone else. He saw no one, but he knew the fire, as warm as it was, as high as the wood was piled, had to have been tended to overnight. He was also covered in a blanket. Someone had put it on him and taken away the remnants of food.

Or maybe it hadn't been someone. Maybe this was an enchanted home. He chuckled to himself. Enchanted home? It sounded like the type of thing Celine would have said. She always believed in those things — old magic, fairytales, sorcerers, and enchanted palaces.

Hmmm, maybe. It made sense, a little. It would explain why he saw no one. It would explain why the things he wanted just appeared.

Whether the house was enchanted or not, he thought he should write a note to tell the owner or enchanter he appreciated the hospitality. He wandered from room to room until he found what appeared to be a study. There were papers, quills and an ink bottle. He took a quill and wrote, "Thank you. Your hospitality to this weary traveler has been remarkable." Then he signed his name and smiled. As he set the note on the desk for the home's master or mistress to find, he noticed something else.

It was a small book with the imprint of a rose on it. It was like the ones Beauty read. He hadn't read them himself. Pierre found the thought of reading anything other than farmer's almanacs a waste of time and logic. But, he knew Beauty enjoyed them. She always smiled when Mme. Giselle brought the volumes. It was definitely the same type of book, only this one looked newer. The leather-bound books Mme. Giselle brought were dark and worn with age. This was lighter toned and in good condition. He opened the flap and saw it was published this year. Oh my, how Beauty would love this.

Pierre decided at that moment that his deceased wife had been right to believe in enchantments. This house was enchanted. It knew what he wanted and provided it to him. Just a moment before, he had wished he had something for Beauty, and then he saw this book. It hadn't been there before; he was sure now. Just as he was setting the note down, he'd thought, "Oh, if only I had something of this experience to show Beauty."

He decided he'd do one last test. I want money, a bag of gold so that I don't have to sell my daughter to that M. Dumas. He closed his eyes, opened them again. Nothing.

Perhaps the house wasn't enchanted after all. He was ready to turn and leave when he glanced out the study's window and saw the garden below. His mouth fell open. Pierre blinked, not sure he could believe what he saw. He closed his eyes and opened them once more. He stepped around the desk, walked right up to the window, pressing his face against the cold window. Yes, down below him was a garden of gold. A garden of solid gold flowers. He was sure of it. He grabbed the book from the desk. This place was enchanted, and he would take the book and some flowers back to his daughter.

Pierre found his way outside to the garden, and when he got there, he confirmed what he'd seen from the window: the flowers were gold. Solid gold. He touched one in awe, and it felt soft, like a flower, yet it was gold. He cut two branches of gold roses and stuck them in his bag. Surely this would pay off his debt to Dumas and keep his daughter safe with him. She wouldn't have to leave him.

He smiled and ran toward the stable, the heft of the gold flowers weighing him down less than it should have because his heart was now light.

He untied the horse from the post and bade it to come on. "We are rich," he said to the horse. That is when Pierre felt pain crushing his shoulder. He turned and first saw the hairy hand clutching him tight. He heard the voice next. It sounded like the growl of a bear, but it was speaking words. "Thief," the voice said, and the furry hand — er, now it looked to him more like a claw — shoved Pierre to the ground.

Pierre turned and looked up. Standing over him was a creature on two legs, dressed in clothes, but covered in fur, like an animal. Its fur was jet black, it had claw-like fingers and sharp teeth. "Thief," it said again. "I give you hospitality, and you steal from me. My book. My flowers."

"No," Pierre was saying, shaking his head. "No. I didn't know," he said. He tried to look the creature in the eye, but it frightened him too much.

"You will die for your crime," the beast said.

The beast's massive, furry hands grabbed hold of Pierre's arm and dragged him away. Pierre tried to loosen the beast's grip, but nothing could pry this thing off of him. "Please, wait, no. I have a daughter. I have a daughter," Pierre begged. The beast didn't seem to care. He dragged Pierre toward a stump, and next to the stump lay an axe. This was a simpler setup than a guillotine, but Pierre knew what was coming next. With no other choice, he pleaded the only thing he thought might earn him mercy. "If you kill me, my daughter will be married off to a cruel tyrant. I must go home. I must repay my debts or my sweet, kind daughter will be doomed."

The beast tossed Pierre to the ground, his eyes cold and merciless, and snarled, "Tell me everything."

Pierre knew this was his only hope, so he confessed to everything — his debt, the cruelness of M. Dumas, how he had promised his daughter to this man, how the gold would help him stop this man, how his daughter had been reading these books and loved them. How he had only taken them because he thought it would hurt no one, that it was an enchanted manor for the weary traveler lucky enough to find it.

The beast listened and finally said, "You are free to go."

The relief surged through Pierre. He couldn't believe it. "Really?"

"Yes," he said. "Take the flowers and pay your debt. You may take more if you feel the need. Take the book to your daughter, and tell her that in one week I will send a carriage for her. She will come live with me forever."

Pierre gasped. "No," he said, shaking his head. "I didn't say that. I'm not giving you my daughter."

The beast laughed in a snarl. "You were going to give her to a tyrant, but you won't give her to me, a creature who shares her interests, and who can provide well for her here?"

Pierre just stared. Yes, this was a nice place, but he couldn't give his daughter to this … this … thing. "I," he started. "You can't have her."

The beast grabbed Pierre by the shoulder and shoved him onto the chopping block. "Very well," said the beast. "I shall kill you and go find her anyway." The beast picked up the axe and lifted it over his head.

"No," Pierre said, his survival instinct outweighing all others. "No, you can have her. I agree to the deal. Please don't kill me."

The beast stepped back from the chopping block and dropped the axe to the ground. "You are right. This house is enchanted," the beast said. "So am I. I will send for your daughter in a week's time. Do not think you can run or hide from me. If you try to run, I will find you. Then, I will kill you and take the girl anyway. Do you understand me?"

Pierre nodded, and he knew in his heart what the beast was saying was true.

"Go now," the beast said. Then, he turned and started walking toward the manor. Pierre got on his horse to ride home. How ever was he going to explain this to Beauty?

3

Pierre was lost in thought the entire ride home. He let the horse find its way back to their little cottage, while he determined exactly how he would tell Beauty what he had done. When Pierre arrived, Beauty was surprised to see him. Pierre sat her in the chair again, and this time he told her the truth. He left nothing out. He told her about his debt, Dumas' cruelty, his plan to try to figure it out later, his encounter with the beast, and his promise to give Beauty to the beast.

The girl's face was red with fury, and in that instant, she looked more like her mother than he had ever recalled.

"So, you've traded me from one beast to another?" she asked, her voice filled with hurt. "Father, how could you?"

He cast his eyes down. "I'm sorry, Beauty," he said. "I wouldn't have done it if he weren't going to kill me."

Beauty took a deep breath and nodded. She tried not to cry. This vile creature who had almost killed her father was to be the man — no the thing — she would spend the rest of her days with. She wasn't sure she could breathe. Dumas' cruelty, so far, had been confined to his business dealings. Perhaps his cruelty was limited to that. But this beast, that was something else altogether. The beast had tried to kill her father and now he wanted her to be with him.

She closed her eyes and lay her head back on the chair's soft cushioned headrest. She felt like crying, but that wouldn't help. She had been lucky growing up, lucky that her father had prized her company and had not forced her to work in the fields. He had her educated with books and encouraged her curiosity. He had done all this at great expense to himself, and was now in debt because of it. So, maybe it was only fair that she was responsible for fixing it.

She took a deep breath, opened her eyes and looked at the book in her lap. "He had this book in his study?" she asked her father. She was repeating the question. She'd asked it before. Normally, she wouldn't question her father, but today she'd learned he was a liar. He'd lied to her about Dumas, and now she felt the need to have him repeat his answers just to see if they held true. She watched his face as he prepared to answer, looking for any signs that he was lying about this.

"Yes," Pierre said, nodding. "I found it in the study. But, I don't know if it is his," he said, looking at the book. "I told you I thought the house was enchanted, that it knew my desires and would make them come true. So, I wished that I had something to bring you. That's when the book appeared."

She frowned. The book probably wasn't even the creature's. The book had appeared because her father wanted a gift for her. Beauty did want to cry now. This beast was probably as monstrous on the inside as he looked on the outside. She looked down at the book, almost hating it now. It had given her ideas, ideas that she knew were wrong, ideas about sins of the flesh and just how pleasurable they could be. She had a Bible, and she and her father went to church once a month for mass. She'd heard the sermons against carnal sins, but she'd ignored them, assuming that something that felt so right when she read it couldn't be wrong. But now she realized she had been fooled. This was her punishment for enjoying these books, for wanting to feel the way the women in these books felt, for touching herself and wanting to be touched that way. Her punishment was life shackled in marriage to a beast.

4

The week passed with Beauty not speaking much to her father. Beauty had told her father that she understood and forgave him. She'd said it because that was the thing she was supposed to say to him, to lessen his feelings of guilt. And part of her did understand. If her life were in danger, would she not have made the same agreement? Probably. But she dreaded being handed over to this beast. He would not be a man like in her books. He wouldn't be able to hold and caress her and treat her kindly.

And if he felt she stole something from him, would he murder her? The way he'd threatened to murder her father? She didn't know, and that scared her. Part of her felt she should hate her father for what he had done to her, for promising her to this thing. Only, the truth was, she would have to be married to someone. That was the way of the world, the way of things. She had even been looking forward to it. But now, fear replaced that yearning. Fear that he would be as beastly with her as he had been with her father. Fear that he would be a brute who took her at will, rather than caressed and held her. Fear that he would become violent and angry.

Even though she was afraid, she had to go. Her fate had been sealed, so she went about preparations to leave. She taught her father to cook a few of the dishes he enjoyed. She'd always cooked for him, and she worried he'd have trouble getting along without her.

If only her father had told her his financial problems sooner, perhaps they could have looked for a different solution, something that would not have involved promising her to a suitor who was a beast.

Beauty packed her meager belongings into a large trunk. It had been her mother's, the one her mother had brought from her family

14

home to her marital home.

Celine had come from a respectable family and had been expected to marry someone of the same station, but she fell in love with Pierre and ran off with him. They had lived more modestly than Celine had been used to, but she had been happy, as far as Beauty knew. It seems, her mother's station had been supporting them since her brothers died. Pierre had sold Celine's jewelry. As a child, Celine's father had lavished expensive baubles on his daughter, and the grownup Celine had brought them all when she ran off with Pierre. Even then, Celine had known, they'd come in handy. There was no jewelry left now, no remnants of the house that Celine had hailed from, no treasures that Beauty could have received from her mother and passed on to her own daughter.

Beauty cringed at the thought. Now, she would have no daughters. At least she didn't think it would be possible to have a child with such a creature. And if it were possible, would the children look like little mutts? She really felt like crying this time. What had her father done to her?

What if she just refused to go? Just then, she heard the whinnying of a horse outside. It was loud and strange, a feral whinny unlike anything she'd ever heard before.

She ran to the door and slung it open. There in front of the house was a carriage, pulled by a horse but with no driver. She walked up to the carriage and looked inside. In shadow, she saw a figure, a hulking figure under a cape. "Get in," it said. The voice was a growl, low and stern, and Beauty's heart sank. Was this to be her life? What if she didn't get in?

"Get in," the voice said again.

"But I want to say goodbye to my father. He went into town to pay M. Dumas. He'll be back shortly."

"Get in," the beast said again.

Beauty looked back at the house. She'd left the door open. "My things," she said. "I need to get my trunk."

"You need nothing. Get in. Now."

His voice was clear and commanding, and something about it made her feel she must obey it. She nodded and climbed into the carriage. She sat down on the bench opposite the beast, looked out the carriage window and watched her house disappear behind her. She turned back to him, to ask him what next, and gasped. He was gone. She reached her hand over to the other side and felt the empty seat. There was nothing there. She looked on the floor, wondering if he could have hidden. But there was no place to hide. She decided to flee the carriage, and tried to open the door, but it wouldn't move. It was locked.

Her father had said the beast lived in an enchanted manor. He had been right. She was afraid now. The beast had been here and disappeared. He had locked her in, made her leave without saying goodbye to her father. Made her leave all her things. Now it was time to cry. She leaned over in her seat and let the tears flow.

5

Beauty lay slumped in tears for the remainder of the carriage ride. This would be her purge. She would cry it out here, and then she would go meet her fate with good cheer. Or at least with the realization that there was nothing she could do to change it. She was bent over, her head resting on her arms, still sniffling onto her sleeves when she realized the carriage had stopped. She sat up, dried her tears, and looked out the carriage window.

Before her was a huge manor, three stories tall and made of stone. It had a small rounded tower on the top left corner. It was so big and so immaculate it reminded her of a church, or a palace. Those were the only buildings that got such care and beauty when built. The sun was setting, and the building looked luminous, bathed in the orange glow of twilight.

This would be OK, she told herself. Instinctively, she looked around to gather her things to take with her, but she had no things to gather. The beast had made her leave with nothing, nothing but the dress she wore. It was one of her mother's old dresses. Not one of the nicer ones — a red, one piece dress that had a decorative ribbon tied around the waist. Apparently, her father had sold the nicest ones for money, to keep them alive and eating for as long as they had. She wished he'd worked harder on farming the vineyard, on earning money there, instead of selling her mother's things. Only, how could she say that? She had been there, and she hadn't insisted on finding out about the finances or offering to help him. Instead, she'd gladly accepted his suggestions to read more and enjoy long walks nearby. She hadn't bothered to wonder how they afforded their lives, when the weather had not been good the past two years. The grapes had done poorly. The ones that had thrived were magnificent, but most

17

hadn't thrived.

So here she was, with nothing but the dress on her back, being sent to be the wife of this beast. She took a deep breath, pushed the carriage door open and descended onto the path that led to the front door. As she approached the door, navigating two small steps to reach it, it swung open by itself. She stopped, startled by the magic that was another confirmation that this place was enchanted. Hearing of it was one thing, but seeing it in person was frightening.

She continued on, entering the house, slightly apprehensive. After she went through the door, it closed on its own. The entryway was dark. There was a chandelier above, but it wasn't lit. She wished it would brighten up, and suddenly the candles of the chandelier sprung to life, flickering gently above her.

She walked further in, and to her right there was a doorway to another room. It was large, and had a fireplace with a roaring fire, some chairs and a sofa. This must be the room her father had fallen asleep in. It was as he described it. Large and warmed by the fire that roared quietly in the hearth.

She went to the chair that had a table beside it and looked for a plate of food, wondering if she would have the same experience as her father. But, when she walked over to the chair with the little table next to it, there was an empty silver serving plate set on the table. No food. She frowned. From behind her, she heard, "Beauty?" The voice was low, but gruff, almost like a growl.

She blew out, squeezed her hands tight, mentally bracing herself for what she'd find when she turned around. Beauty turned slowly and kept her lips clamped shut, so she didn't gasp. What she saw was a large creature. He stood on two legs, but he was as large as a black bear. He was clothed like a man, like a well-dressed, respectable gentleman, a fancy blue overcoat, black britches, and a decorative cravat. But everything that wasn't clothed was covered in fur, thick black fur. His face had bestial qualities, his mouth sticking out slightly, like it was a snout, but not quite as long as any animal's snout. When he opened his mouth to smile, she saw his fine, sharp teeth, the kind that would frighten anyone daring to get into a fight with him. Though, she couldn't imagine anyone sane trying to fight with this creature. He was muscular — it shown through his clothes, the way he was stuffed into them, the way they practically burst off of him. Not the way fat, slovenly people's clothes didn't fit. He was well defined and toned. She couldn't help but look down and notice he wore no shoes. Probably because his feet were like paws. Long and thick with pointed claws at the ends. His hands were similar, but on a smaller scale, probably more human in look, but with unkempt nails.

"Beauty?" the creature said again.

She couldn't find her voice just yet, so she nodded her head and looked into his eyes. And that was the thing that struck her. While the rest of him seemed some combination of beast and man, his eyes, dark brown and deep with wonder, were completely human. There was something about them that pulled you to them and made you want to draw closer to him, even though everything else about him said you shouldn't. She stared into those deep brown eyes and wondered how he came to be this way. Was his mother human and his father an animal? Had he been cursed — or enchanted — by this house? Who was he — this creature with eyes that said there was so much more to him than what was on the surface?

"You may call me Beast," he said, approaching her, trying to look friendly with a smile. Though it was impossible for him to succeed at looking friendly with long, sharp fangs jutting from his mouth. "Did your father explain the terms of your being here?"

Beauty nodded. "I am to be your wife and stay here with you."

The beast chuckled, a sound that began with a growl and ended in a luscious, yet airy howl. "Maybe that is how your father looked at it," he said. "You do not have to be my wife." Beauty was surprised by this, but she just kept her mouth shut and watched, waiting for him to continue. "Your only obligation is to stay here with me, forever. If you want more, I would like that, but I won't force you. The important thing is that you must stay here. You don't get to leave."

Beauty stared at him, trying to comprehend. "I don't get to leave?" she asked. "I'm confined to this house?" She could not hide the alarm in her voice. The idea of being stuck inside all the time, of not going out, even if for a walk to see the birds swoop through the air or the ants build a little hill, frightened her.

"You can go anywhere on the grounds. The property is four acres. But, not beyond that. You must stay here on the estate."

Beauty breathed out, slightly relieved. She could go outside, explore the grounds. That was better than nothing, but that hardly seemed enough. "My father," she said. "May I go see him, or go back home to collect my things?"

Beast shook his head. "You must stay here."

Beauty frowned. She'd have preferred a forced marriage, where she could occasionally leave to see her family, to the arrangement he was describing. She was stuck here with this beast until she died, and she could visit no one or talk to no one. "And if I refuse?" she asked. She thought she knew the answer, but she wanted to hear him say it.

"Your father and I agreed he could take enough gold to pay his debts and I would spare his life, if you came here to live. If you refuse, then his agreement with me would be null and void. I would claim his life, and his heirs, you, would have to repay me the worth of the gold he took. As I understand, he's already spent it. Do you have means to repay the gold?"

His voice had been monotone through most of his little message, but at the end, when he asked his question, he stared at her bosoms and grinned.

"It doesn't matter," Beauty said, flushing lightly as he continued to stare at her chest. "I do not refuse. I will stay here with you."

Beast nodded. "Let me show you to your room," he said as he turned and walked out of the room, not looking back. He clearly assumed she'd follow, so she hurried behind him as he went back into the main hallway. She turned her head and briefly looked at the front door, wondering if it would open to allow her out. If it did, could she escape? Even if she did get out, he would come for her father, and then for her to repay the gold.

She turned back to Beast, followed him up a beautiful marble staircase, and turned right at the top. They walked down a long hallway, past a few doors, and then to one on the right. He opened the door and motioned for her to go in. She walked past him and into a peach-colored room, with a large canopy bed in the center. There were several windows in the room, letting in the remains of the day's light. She imagined it would be bright and sunny at the start of the day. The drapes were open, but she could easily close them if she wanted darkness to sleep late. There was an ornately carved bureau, some plush chairs, a dressing table, and other accoutrements that she'd read that the wealthy have in their homes. Only, she'd never actually seen such things with her own eyes. It was much nicer than the little home she shared with her father. Only, at this moment, she felt keenly homesick for her tiny featherbed on the floor, and the coziness of curling up on it with one of Ferus Lucunditas' volumes.

She turned to see Beast staring at her. He seemed to be waiting for her, perhaps for her to say something. "Thank you," she said. He nodded, though he'd seemed to want her to say more. "Are there clothes?" she asked.

"Yes," he said. "In the wardrobe, there are some dresses I thought you would like. But those are my tastes. If there is anything you want, just think it, and it will appear."

Beauty's mouth popped open. She'd known the house was enchanted, but she hadn't expected it to be so easy to control. "Just think it?"

"Yes," he said, as he walked closer to her. He stopped right in front of her, his barrel chest almost touching her bosoms. He closed his eyes and held his hand out to the side. A moment later, a book appeared on his palm. He grinned and offered it to Beauty. She looked down at the book: Volume 18 by Ferus Lucunditas. "I thought you might like this. Perhaps we could read it together," he said, raising an eyebrow. As he stared, it felt as if he were undressing her with his eyes. As if he were imagining taking off the dress she wore and the simple chemise she wore underneath it, to stare at her naked body.

Beauty took a step back, but did not take the book. She stared at it, knowing the kind of story it held. One about a couple that yearns to touch each other, a couple who has a spark between them, the air practically humming with a quiet electricity when they are close. A hum that can only be muted by passionate, all-encompassing sex. She watched him look at her as if he were trying to make them connect, trying to make the air between them hum. For a second, she felt it, the gentle pull toward him, and a whiff of his musky scent that seemed to say he wanted her. And then she stopped herself.

She was angry, because she felt this was some type of trick. The beast thought that because her father had tried to take one of those books for her that Beauty read them and enjoyed them. He thought that because she enjoyed those tales, he could have his way with her. He'd pretended downstairs that she had a choice. He'd said her only obligation was to stay, that she didn't have to do more if she didn't want more. But she realized now there was no choice. His eyes spoke the desire of his loins as they watched her greedily. She looked down and could see the burgeoning lump in his pants.

"You pretend I have a choice," she said. "But, I know what you want. You can take it, because I can't stop you, but please stop pretending I have a say. You want what you want, and you plan to take it."

Beast's nostrils flared, and the desire in his eyes turned to anger. For a moment, she thought he would strike her, that he would be cruel, that he would be the beast that he looked like. Instead, he leaned in close to her, placing a hairy finger on her shoulder blade near the neckline of her dress. He slid his finger down her flesh, following the curve of the neckline, which made a V intersection at her breasts. His finger lingered on the left breast a moment, and then he made a circular motion that sent tingles through Beauty. No one had ever touched her like that before, and it made her warm in all the right places. He slid his soft, hairy finger to the other breast, back up the neckline of the dress, to her neck, which he caressed lightly. Beauty found her breaths becoming shallower as he did this, the light tickling sensation making it hard for her to think clearly.

Beast leaned into her ear and whispered, "I will not touch you again without your permission. I will not talk to you about the books again, unless you ask me. I will not pleasure you from head to toe like Marat Rossini does to Helena in Volume 3, unless you ask me. But, when you do ask me, know that I will. I will do it, as much as you want, as long as you want, over and over and over again, if you want. There's nothing wrong with me wanting to pleasure you, or you wanting to pleasure me."

Beast took a step back, removing his fingers from Beauty's skin. The spot he'd been touching still felt hot. It felt almost as if the heat from that spot could grow and consume the rest of Beauty's body. It had left her alight with desire, but she didn't want to show it. Beauty could tell her face was red, and her expression was still shocked. She watched as he turned and left the room without another word.

6

Beast stormed back to his room and closed the door with a thud that was harder than he'd intended. He wanted her to think he was in control, that he was able to master himself, to not hurt her, to not take what he wanted.

Only, he wasn't sure he was. It had taken every bit of constructive will within himself not to rip her clothes off, throw her on the bed and take her. He'd imagined it. From the moment he saw her, with her straight auburn hair flowing to just beneath her shoulders, and her beautiful breasts tempting him from within that dress. Why was the neckline so low? He was sure her breasts beneath it were beautiful and round, like grapefruits, with gorgeous pink areolas that he could suckle. And when he did, she would moan with pleasure. She had wide, tempting hips, and he wanted nothing more than to grab them and hold them tight as he slid right into her and pounded her until she could take no more, until she cried out in pleasure that she wanted him to come. He wanted her. He wanted her more than he had wanted anyone, and he wanted her now.

He shook his head, closed his eyes, and took a deep breath. He couldn't do that. He just couldn't. That would mean he hadn't changed. All these years, he'd been confined to this estate would have been a waste if he hadn't changed. He thought he'd become enlightened, learned his lesson, and was someone who could want a woman who didn't want him and not let it bother him. But it wasn't true. He wanted her, more than he'd ever wanted anyone. More than he'd wanted Isabelle. Beautiful, beautiful Isabelle, the pretty, shy girl that every boy wanted. Hair the color of straw, large round breasts, and a full rump. But he wasn't every boy. He was a Verran, and all the girls wanted to be with boys from the Verran family. He was 18 and had bedded more of the town's pretty girls than he could count. They threw themselves at him, hoping he would fall for them, hoping he would take them and be so enamored that he'd marry them. Marry them and they'd gain access to the Verran fortune.

Getting girls had always been easy. He didn't care that he left some heartbroken. He would always buy them something special, usually a rose and a trinket, and then tell them it was over. But Isabelle. She had been different. She'd been beautiful, of course. All the girls had been beautiful. But Isabelle had played hard to get. She had pretended she wasn't interested. It just made his passion all the more wild. He pursued her relentlessly, and she continued to deny him.

Finally one night, when most of the town was at the winter ball, he cornered Isabelle in the stables where she liked to tend to the animals. He told her it was time to stop playing, that she would finally be his. She told him no, but he knew it was just more of her playing, more playing designed to drive him insane with lust, so he pushed her down on a bed of hay intended for the animals and began to tear her clothes off, even as she begged him to stop. He was about to rip off her undergarments when she said something he'd never heard before, something so strange to his ears, that even now he couldn't reproduce the sound. It was like a primordial cry. And then, behind him, he heard a thud, and in walked a woman in a red, hooded cloak. He couldn't see her face, obscured by the hood, but he could see her eyes were red like a demon. The eyes scared him so much that he turned away, back at Isabelle, who was in tears, flanked by the shreds of her dress. It only occurred to him, then, at that very moment, that she had not been playing, that she really did not want him, and he felt sorry that he hadn't seen it. He said her name like a question, "Isabelle?" In his mind, it was a question. He wondered, was that really her? Had he really caused her to cry like that?

"Don't you dare!" said a voice behind him, and he turned back to see the cloaked woman standing before him. "Don't you dare say this sweet girl's name again, not after what you tried to do to her. I've watched her for a long time from afar, because I thought she was kind, and I knew you were no good. I told her if ever she was in trouble to call for me, and, thankfully, she did. You are a vile, vile human being for trying to hurt her."

"I'm sorry," he said. Even now, seven years later, he wasn't sure if he had meant that he was sorry for what he had tried to do to the girl or if he was just frightened of the creature's wrath. He didn't know if the creature was a devil or sorceress or both.

"You're sorry you got stopped," the woman hissed, "Not sorry for what you did." She looked at Isabelle, and said, "Encampe maison." The girl disappeared. His heartbeat quickened. This woman was definitely an evil sorceress.

"Please," he said. "Please, I'm sorry. I thought she was just teasing. Please don't hurt me. Please have mercy on me."

Before that moment, he had never begged for anything from anyone. He had always been given what he wanted, or taken it, if it wasn't offered. He had always felt entitled to it, the way he'd felt entitled to Isabelle. But, he knew in that moment, as he stood in the shadow of this woman, that he was entitled to nothing. Not even life. He feared she would kill him. Some days, he wished she had killed him.

Instead, she cursed him. "You are a beast, and everyone will know it by looking at you."

He stared at her, confused, and waited a moment for her to say something more, but she didn't. The fear that was paralyzing him moments earlier trickled away as he realized that she was all bark without bite. He laughed. "That's it?" he said. "You call me a beast and say everyone will know it."

"Your fear turns to hubris too easily," she said. "Look at your hands."

He looked down, and though he'd felt no change, his hands were covered in fur. He looked down at his legs. They were still in his pants, but his feet, somehow without him noticing, had broken through his shoes and were now giant paws, with clawed toes. He reached up and felt his face. It was covered in hair. His ears were now pointy, like a wolf's. He felt his nose and mouth; they had morphed into something larger, like a snout. "What did you do to me?" he asked, wishing there were a mirror, wishing he could see himself.

She laughed, her whole frame shaking as her cruel cackle left her hood. "You will remain a beast until you learn how to control yourself."

"I can," he said. "I can do that now. I won't ever do anything like this again. I promise." He got onto his knees. "Please," he said.

"Please take it back. Please undo this sorcery."

The hood shook from side-to-side, only the red eyes visible. "Only you can undo this."

"How?" he begged, "Please, tell me how."

"You must learn to control yourself, and you must convince another that you are worthy of her love, despite your appearance."

He could do that. He would go home and tell one of the girls he'd been with what had happened. She would profess her love, and this curse would end. He was sure he could convince someone to love him, even if it was just the love of his status as a Verran.

There was a snarl from the woman. "You are so transparent," she said. "Reading your thoughts is like finding the moon on a cloudless night. Too easy."

He looked up at her, confused.

"You think your name, your status, will save you?"

His mouth fell open. She actually had read his mind.

"Emile de Verran, from now on, you will be called Beast. I suggest you tell no one your real name, for if they call you by your real name, it will be catastrophic."

He waited for her to say more. She didn't. He wanted to grab her and ring her neck, but he knew her magic was too powerful for him to counter. Why would she curse him to this beastly form and then play word riddles with him? "How will it be catastrophic? What will happen?"

She smiled. "It is not so funny when people play with your feelings, is it, Beast?" she said, as if she had searched his mind and seen all the cruelty he had exhibited toward his former lovers. And, yes, it was cruel of him to lead them on, he realized just then. The woman spoke. "If someone calls you by your name, you, Beast, shall die. You must convince someone to love you with only your personality. And it cannot be the shallow love of schoolgirl crushes. It must be time-tested and long-endured, the love of truth and unity."

What the Hell did that even mean? A love of truth and unity. He was lost.

"I am sending you away now," the sorceress said.

His eyes widened. "What?"

"You will be sent to an enchanted manor. Everything you need to live will be provided for you. But you will not be able to leave the grounds. If you do, you will die."

26

"Then how am I to find a girl to love me?"

She laughed again, another wicked cackle. "I guess that does present a dilemma, doesn't it? I'm sure you'll figure it out."

The arms of the cloak rose high as if she were doing a spell, Beast saw a bright light, and then he was here. He'd been here for the last seven years. And now he had his chance. He had to make Beauty love him, and he had to control himself.

7

That night, Beauty had a dream. In it, Beast came into her room, where Beauty was lying in bed naked. Beast lay next to her and stared. His eyes drank her in greedily, but he didn't touch her.

She wasn't sure why she was naked, but she wanted him to touch her. She wanted him to glide his fingers along her breasts. She wanted him to kiss her, to know what it felt like to have his mouth on hers. She wanted him to pull her close to him so she knew what if felt like to have her body pressed against his. Only, he did nothing but watch. It drove her mad at the same time it pleased her. Pleased her to have him so close, but aggravated her that he wouldn't do what they both seemed to want.

"Why do you just stare?" she asked, and her words sounded more like a plea than a question.

"Because you haven't asked," he said simply.

She stared at him, not sure she should ask, but realizing she couldn't take the agony of wanting him any longer. "Kiss me," she said.

He sat up, then climbed on top of her, straddling her naked body with his clothed body. She was startled by what this did to her, how it made her feel down below: moist, warm and yearning for more. He smiled at her, then leaned forward, pressing his lips to hers, sliding his tongue into her mouth. It wrapped with hers, doing a seductive dance. She liked the feel of his mouth on hers, the scent of him, so close, a little bit earthy and rustic. She even liked the tickle of his facial hair against her chin. His mouth stayed pressed to hers, their tongues mingling, and she felt short of air, but she didn't care. She wanted to pull him closer to feel him closer, but he somehow resisted.

He pulled away, stared at her lying beneath him. "Did you like your kiss?"

She nodded.

He smiled crookedly, his brown eyes gleaming. "If you want more, you only have to ask."

She did want more. She opened her mouth to ask, but then she heard a noise, a high-pitched warbling. She turned to see what it was. Then, her eyes popped open. It had been a dream. She was alone in her bed, and there was a bird singing outside her window.

* * *

Beauty didn't want to see Beast, not after that dream. She conjured breakfast in her room, thinking of croissants, fresh fruit and milk. She ate, and then the dishes disappeared when she thought she'd like them gone.

She wanted to explore the house and grounds a little, but not run into him. She went outside to the garden and saw the golden roses. They were magnificent, even prettier in bloom than they were after they'd been cut and stuffed into a bag, as were the first ones she'd seen — the ones her father had brought back.

Beauty was looking at the flowers when she heard the sound of an axe, the clop of cut wood as it was stacked and labored breathing. She rounded the corner of the manor and saw Beast, an axe in his hand, splitting logs for firewood. He wore only trousers, and she could see just how powerful and muscular he was. Even though his skin was covered in thick black fur, she could see the defined pectoral muscles, brawny biceps and toned abdominal muscles. He was strong and powerful, and she wondered what it would feel like to be held in his arms.

He was lifting the axe to chop another log when he spotted her and smiled. He set the axe down and walked over toward her. "Good day to you, Beauty," he said, upon reaching her. She didn't want him to know she was avoiding him, so she forced a smile in response.

"Did you sleep well?" he asked.

She nodded, but again she didn't want to speak. Instead, she stared at him, at just how massive he was up close, just how sculpted his chest was. Perhaps cutting firewood kept his upper body so strong.

"Have you seen the roses?" he asked, his voice a little uncertain, as if he were afraid he were boring her.

She shook her head.

"I'll show them to you," he said, turning toward the garden. He started to hold out his hand toward her, but then, as if suddenly remembering his vow not to touch her again until she asked, he retracted the hand and said, "Follow me."

For some reason, Beauty felt stung by his action, but she didn't know if it stung because she wanted him to touch her and he wouldn't. Or if it stung because she wished she didn't want him to touch her. She followed him to the roses, and they stood next to one of the bushes, a foot or so of space between them. Beast bent a branch with a rose toward her. "Touch it," he suggested. "I think you'll be surprised."

Beauty reached out her hand toward the petal, bringing it within an inch of Beast's hand. She looked at him, and he was watching carefully to see if she would actually touch him. She bit her lower lip and decided not to give him the satisfaction. She felt the rose's petals, and they were soft, like those of a real flower. She actually was startled by how soft they felt. "How is this possible?" she asked. "The flowers my father carried were hard."

Beast smiled. "After they're cut, they turn to regular gold within a few hours, gold that can't grow and breathe, expand, or open its petals, or even wither and die. But, as long as they're growing, they're like real flowers. In need of love and attention, so they can open up and blossom." He looked at her longingly and said, "Sometimes they just need the right touch, the right caress, to bloom."

The air between them was charged, and she felt herself drawn to Beast, drawn to his words, drawn to his sweaty, musky scent after cutting wood. She had to go. She turned and tripped over a rock. She was sure she was going to fall flat on her face and put her hands out in front of her. Instead, she felt Beast's arms wrap around her waist and pull her back to him.

She was clasped against his body, a firm, sweaty, tangle of muscles and fur. Her breath was ragged from the shock of the near fall and the quick rescue. Her heart thumped in her chest. Beast released her. "I'm sorry," he said.

She took two steps away and looked at him. "For what?" she asked.

"I promised not to touch you," he said, looking at her eyes, seeming to beg permission to touch her again. "I only did it to stop your fall."

"I know," she said, but she looked down at the ground. The grass was still green, but not particularly lush, due to the cold.

He stepped closer to her, so close that she could feel his breath on her. "I will keep my promise in the future, so long as you're not in danger of getting hurt. I won't touch you unless you ask."

Beauty looked into his eyes, and it was as if they were demanding she ask him. Demanding her to say, "Please, touch me." Or was it her eyes that were demanding that? Maybe it was another part of her body. The body that felt drawn to his, that wanted to feel him touching her everywhere. "Yes, please don't," she whispered, then turned and walked away.

Beauty managed to avoid Beast. She would watch him chopping wood from her window, telling herself it was because she wanted to know when he finished and came inside. But, part of her liked watching him, liked watching the way his muscles flexed and bent as he slammed the axe down. Liked watching his breath become labored if he was out there a long while. Liked the memory of his musky, earthy scent. She wondered if his sweat would taste salty if she licked it off of him. And then she would have to turn away from her window and remind herself just to look and see if Beast were finished, nothing more. She knew she shouldn't give in to her yearnings with Beast. He wasn't even a man, but she felt the desire to be with him, and it was growing stronger.

She managed to avoid him during the day, but at night she couldn't. He invaded her sleep. She dreamed that Beast came into her room and walked straight across to the bed, where Beauty lay in only a corset, buttoned at the front. He told her he'd changed his mind. He would take her now, if that was alright. Beauty was too stunned to reply, so she watched him with anticipation, her mouth watering at the thought of his touch.

Beast mounted the bed, climbing on top of her, bending over her, his soft warm breath on her neck. The sensation, like a hot breeze caressing her skin, made her shiver with pleasure. She wondered what he would touch next, and if it would make her body react like this. He lifted his head and looked in her eyes. She thought he might kiss her. She imagined how his lips would feel pressed against hers. How his tongue would feel inside her mouth.

But he didn't kiss her. Instead, he lowered his head until he was right over her corset. He put his mouth on the first button, his tongue lightly touching her breast. Then he bit down on the button and Beauty felt his warm lips caress the fabric. He lifted his head, and she felt a slight tugging and realized he'd bitten the button right off. She hadn't realized she'd been holding her breath, anticipating his move, but she had been. She breathed out, a small shocked whoosh. He looked up at her and grinned. Then he bent his head over her corset and did it again and again. Twenty three times, he bit the buttons off the corset. She wanted him to hurry, to get it off, yet she liked to watch the way he ripped the button from her clothing, as if that said something about the passion with which he would take her. When her corset was completely debuttoned, it spread open slightly, exposing a sliver of skin down the center. He used his furry fingers to spread the remains of the garment, exposing her naked breasts, her tummy and the hair that hid her womanhood.

He traced his finger along the areola of each breast, the tingling sensation thrilling her and making her moist. His finger slid over her abdomen, down her hair, and right to the opening of her womanhood. "May I?" he asked, surprising her. She nodded, but he didn't move. "May I?" he asked again.

"Yes," she breathed out, and he plunged his finger into her. His hand was large, and so was his finger, and the sensation of his single finger sliding in and out of her made Beauty's breath catch in her throat. She wanted to focus on the sensation, but she couldn't linger as she felt his tongue on her left nipple. He suckled her as he gently thrust his large finger in and out of her. The pleasure was immense and overriding. She'd never felt anything as good before, and she wanted more. She heard a moan escape her lips, though it wasn't a sound she had ever made before. It sounded beastly, almost. Though, maybe that was appropriate, given who she was with.

He moved his finger inside her faster and faster, and she felt the pleasure building. He grabbed her hair and pulled her head so it tilted back. Then, she felt him suckling her neck, and it felt so good, another wave of pleasure rolled through her. She didn't want him to stop, and she told him so. He didn't stop until she was spent, her body having convulsed with release at least three times. He smiled when they were through. "Did you enjoy that?"

She started to nod, but then remembered he liked to hear her answers. "Yes."

"Good," he said. "Next time, we'll do more."

More, she thought. It had been what Mme. Giselle had said. More. Yes, she wanted more.

That is when Beauty awoke, to learn it had only been a dream. She was alone in her bed chamber, wearing her chemise, rather than a broken corset. Of course, she was moist down below. While she realized it was just a dream, it had felt so real; she wished it had been.

9

The dream he'd had last night, of being with Beauty, had tormented him. The first dream, the one of him lying in her bed and staring at her, had felt like agony, but the one last night had driven him mad. He was sure not even Sisyphus had felt as frustrated. If only the dream had been real, he would at least have felt some relief. But, it was only a dream, and everything in him was pent up and still awaiting release.

He wanted her. He wanted her more than he'd ever wanted Isabelle. He wondered if his desire was augmented by the fact that it had been so long since he'd really been with a woman, not just imagined it. And even in the dream, he hadn't fully been with her. He'd pleasured her, just to see how she liked it, just because he wanted to see how she'd clench around him, how her bosoms would heave when she was excited, how her mouth would form a little O of pleasure. He'd wanted to know what she looked like when she really enjoyed it, what her unbridled pleasure looked like as she orgasmed.

He'd not been disappointed. Not in her reaction. Just in the fact that it was a dream. So vivid it might have been real.

He went downstairs and looked to see if Beauty were awake and roaming the house. He found her at the dining room table. He was pleasantly surprised; earlier, she had been avoiding him. It was a long table, as if it was expected to accommodate a dozen or more dinner guests. Unfortunately, it had always been just Beast. She'd chosen to sit on the end opposite from where Beast normally sat. He could take his usual position or do something different.

He chose to be different, taking a seat to her right. She was eating a plate of scrambled eggs and cheese. It was good that she was getting used to using the house's enchantment. He hoped it meant she was starting to feel at home here. Beast closed his eyes and thought of a cut of steak and eggs. When he opened them, the plate was before him.

He looked at Beauty and started to smile. Then, his mouth dropped open. He should have noticed before. He didn't know why he hadn't. Maybe because dreams are like that — hard to recall until the details slam into you like a wall. But, now he was sure of it. He counted silently, the way he had last night in his dream. Twenty-three. There were 23 buttons on the corset. It was the exact color and fabric of the corset he'd ripped the buttons off of in his dreams.

Beauty was eyeing him curiously, as if she were concerned by his stare.

"Lovely corset," Beast said.

Beauty raised an eyebrow.

"You thought of that, this morning?"

She nodded, but stared at him, as if something about what he was asking were troubling her.

Even though he knew she seemed troubled by it, he had to find out more. It couldn't be coincidence that the corset of his dream was the one she was wearing. He didn't fully understand the enchantment of the house, so he wondered if he was able to dream of her in the corset because she had actually worn it to bed last night. "I know this a strange question," he said. "But, did you sleep in that corset?"

She stood up, nostrils flaring. "Tell me now," she said coldly. "Do the powers you have to enchant this house also allow you to read my mind, to invade my dreams?"

He couldn't help smiling. She had dreamed it, too. "No, I have no power to read minds or invade dreams," he said. He didn't tell her he hadn't enchanted the house. He realized she couldn't find out that he was a prisoner here as much as she was. Or, really, that he was the only prisoner here. That she could leave at any time and he couldn't follow. He needed her to stay long enough that she didn't want to leave. "Even if I had the power at my will, I wouldn't invade your dreams. Our dreams and our thoughts should be private."

She studied his face a moment, then frowned. "Why did you ask about the corset?"

"I had a dream last night that I came into your room and ripped the buttons off your corset. There were 23, just like on this one."

Her face flushed and she took a step back. "I had the same

dream," she said softly.

"I've always lived here alone," Beast said. "Perhaps when there's another person in the house, we somehow share dreams."

She seemed to be mulling it over, pondering whether that could be true. Then she shook her head. "Or perhaps you say that you will not touch me again without my asking and then you invade my dreams to do so."

Beast stood, too, suddenly flooded with anger. He had been nothing but kind to her, and now she was accusing him of being something he wasn't. Something he had been trying to overcome so he could lift this damned curse. "Are you saying I am a liar? That I somehow invaded your dream on purpose, so I could violate my word? So I could take you against your will?"

Beauty paused for a moment, watching him. "I don't know."

"I am not a liar," he said vehemently. "And I will never force you to be in my bed." He picked up his plate of food, then turned to leave the room. "Enjoy your breakfast," he said and then exited.

10

east did not speak to Beauty for several days, and that
bothered her. She hadn't meant to accuse him of being a liar
or trying to have his way with her on the sly. Well, actually, she
supposed she had meant it at the time, but she hadn't meant for him
to take it so hard, or for him to think she didn't believe him when he
said he hadn't.

Everything about being here was hard. She was away from home,
away from things familiar, and she was experiencing new things, too.
This enchanted house, and that dream. That dream had felt so real.
She had wanted it to be real, and that frightened her. She wasn't
supposed to want Beast the way she did. She wasn't supposed to
have those kinds of feelings about a creature that wasn't even a man.
But, she did. She had urges. They were normal, at least that's what
the young women in the Ferus Lucunditas books were always told by
their mothers, or their good married friends. It's normal to have
those urges, to let one's husband fulfill them. But Beast wasn't her
husband or even a man.

Beauty hadn't realized it, but she had a stubborn streak. Her father
had always been kind and generally willing to yield, so she hadn't
exercised that streak. But, with Beast, she felt the need not to give in,
not to yield. It was something she'd never really felt before with
others. She wondered if it was the house causing this, or something
about Beast himself. She wondered if there was some reason she
wanted to seem unyielding to him. Or maybe that was just it. She
wanted to yield to him. She wanted to yield to his every desire, but
she was afraid to tell him. Afraid what he'd think of her if she
acquiesced to his desires so soon. Yes, they were natural desires, but
despite what she'd read from Mr. Lucunditas, she'd also heard the

other girls talk about being coy, mastering the chase, and not making yourself too available. Though, this was all talk of finding a suitor, one who might petition your father for your hand. Beauty hadn't gotten to see these girls often, for she hadn't gone into town much, so maybe the snippets of conversation she'd heard had been wrong or out of context or misconstrued.

She wasn't sure what she was doing. She was here with Beast. Forever. But the fact that he had given her a choice, a choice of whether he could touch her, a choice of whether she wanted to be his wife, made her think she shouldn't choose too quickly. That she should pause and not give into desires immediately. If you were given a choice in something, it was wise to weigh all the options, to figure out what the best one was.

Perhaps that was it. Perhaps that was why she was so reluctant to say yes to Beast, so angry when he invaded her dreams. It was as if he were rushing her in a choice that had to be hers. He was trying to seduce her into choosing him, when she needed to make her choice separate from the seduction. The other problem was, she wanted to be seduced. But, perhaps that was the rub of it all. Perhaps that was why she hated it so. She had no choice. Her only choice had been whether to come here at all or to let Beast kill her father. Did it matter if she said she'd be his wife or not? If he came to her in dreams, the way he had the other night, soon she would let him take her. She already wanted it.

Beauty shook her head and sighed. She was sitting in a chair not far from the fireplace in the main room. She wanted a book. Something funny. A moment later, a book appeared on the table next to her. She picked it up, and then heard a noise. She turned to see that Beast had walked in. He stared at her a moment, and she wondered if he would turn around and walk out. That is what he had done the past several days.

"I'm sorry," she said, before he could leave the room. "I shouldn't have accused you of lying, and I should have believed you when you said you didn't invade my dream on purpose."

A look of relief swept his animal face, his snout looking less tight, and the change it produced made him seem less animal, more human.

"I accept your apology," he said, walking closer to her, then finally sitting in a chair across from her. "I shouldn't have behaved so childishly the past few days because my feelings were hurt. You don't

Rosetta Bloom

know me. So, I shouldn't have expected you to believe me."

"You're right," Beauty said, running her fingers across the book in her hand. "I don't know you, and if we're going to be here together, in this house, on the grounds, I should get to know you. We should get to know each other."

Beast nodded.

"Honestly," Beauty added. "We should get to know each other honestly."

Beast frowned, and squished his eyebrows together. "I haven't lied to you," Beast said.

Beauty took a deep breath. "I imagine you haven't. But, I've lied to you, sort of." Beast looked surprised, as if he couldn't imagine Beauty lying about anything. "I've been pretending I don't want to try having relations with you, that it's been all you, all you invading my dreams and lusting after me," she said, pausing, not sure she wanted to admit the truth, but feeling obligated to tell him, since she'd said she'd be honest. "I … I do want you. I'm just afraid. I've never been with a man before. And you're, you're," she looked at him and realized she couldn't say a beast, nor could she say a man. "You're more than a man. You're different, and it frightens me to say yes to something I have no idea about with someone who is so unlike anyone I've ever met or read about."

Beast leaned forward, took her hand. "I know it must be frightening to be in this situation, with someone like me, but I promise you, I will be gentle with you. Like in the dream."

"And if we did that, my choice would be made?" Beauty asked. "I would be your wife."

Beast smiled, and shook his head. "You would have what you wanted if we were intimate, but you would only be my wife if you wanted to be."

"So, being with you in the bedroom wouldn't mean we were married?"

Beast sighed. "No. Marriage is about a true, uniting love. Only if we had that, would we be married."

Beauty nodded, looked deep into his brown eyes, leaned in and kissed him. The electricity she felt was immediate when her lips touched his, like a bolt of lightning had run through her. His mouth opened and his tongue slid in, their breath mingling together, causing Beauty to feel tingly all over. She pulled back, breathless. It had been a good kiss, and she'd hardly noticed the furriness of his face during it. He was a beast, but he was gentle in so many ways. She stood and turned to leave the room.

Beast stood, confused. "Where are you going?"

She turned back to him. "We," she said, elongating the eeee, "are going upstairs, and you are going to help me experience the passion I've only read about until now."

Beast's lips parted as if in shock. "Right now?" he said, more statement than question.

Beauty quirked her ruby red lips up into a smirk. "Unless you have another pressing engagement you must attend to."

Beast strode toward her, shook his head. "No," he said, lifting her off her feet and carrying her up the stairs. "I've got hours and hours of free time."

Beauty blushed, not sure she could handle that, but gladly willing to try.

11

Unwilling to put Beauty down to open the door, Beast kicked it open, the door swinging precariously on its hinges and smacking the wall behind the door.

He carried Beauty to the bed, and laid her gently in the center of it. He climbed on top of her, just as she had remembered it from the dream, straddling her, and bent over toward her corset. She anticipated him leaning over, gently biting off each button. But, this time he didn't. He took his massive hands, grabbed each side of the corset and ripped it apart.

She looked at the tattered corset, feeling slightly alarmed. "I thought you were going to be gentle," Beauty said.

"I will be gentle with you," Beast said, smiling. "But not with your clothing."

Beauty found the thought of him shredding her clothes so he could get to her more quickly incredibly sexy. She loved the passion and the expediency of it. It was even practical, as she was fully dressed, wearing a chemise under the corset, as well as a petticoat, and skirt. If Beast lingered as long as he had in the dream with every strap and button … well, she didn't think she could wait that long. He ripped open her chemise, then tore open her skirt with his teeth. He seemed to need her right now, and was moving at an inhuman speed to accomplish that, for Beauty was now naked, less than a minute after he'd ripped off her corset.

Then he pulled his own clothes off. In a couple of swift motions, he was naked, and she couldn't help but be dazzled as she looked at him. Yes, he was furry, but he was still like a man in so many ways. He had nipples protruding from his chest, from all that hair. You could tell he was strong, by the muscular arms and toned abdomen.

And then of course, there was the *piece de resistance*, the thing she'd not seen on a real, live actual man: a penis. She'd seen them on farm animals, pigs and bulls. But not on a man, yet he wasn't really quite a man, Beast. His cock was flesh colored, probably the color of his skin beneath all his fur, and it was long and thick like a cucumber. She could tell it was hard and ready to pump, and the sight of it made her wetter with anticipation. Part of her wondered if she'd be able to accommodate it because it seemed so big. But, the other part of her looked forward to trying, looked forward to seeing how well he fit inside her.

Beauty licked her lips. Beast stared at her, focusing on her breasts, round and plump with pink nipples and slightly darker areola. She watched as he took his pointer finger and traced it across both nipples, ringing around the areola. She watched as her nipples grew in size, hardening. His fingers slowly left her breasts, tracing down the center of her belly, down further, to her abdomen, and then through the thick, curly auburn hair of her ladyhood. The hair was a little darker than the hair on her head, and he seemed to be staring at it. Beauty's legs had been shut, her thighs touching, but Beast slid his hand into the area, and she instinctively popped them open, so he could get access.

He traced his finger through her hair and down into her opening. She watched him, a smile on her lips the whole time, until he slid his thick finger in her. That's when she closed her eyes and embraced the pleasure. She was already slick with wetness, and the feel of him as he slid a finger inside her was breathtaking. She gasped and breathed out as the walls of her love contracted around his finger. It was seductive, but she knew it wasn't all there was. She wanted, more. The more Giselle had told her about. The more Beast had promised in the dream last night.

As if sensing her desire, Beast withdrew his finger, leaned over and licked her neck. The sensation of his long tongue swiping across her neck caused a tremor of bliss. She breathed out seductively, and it was as if she had ignited a fire within Beast. His mouth seemed to be everywhere, her neck, her breasts, suckling them, teasing her nipples, tracing her belly. His hands were like tentacles, managing to caress her along her sides and back and bottom. It created fantastic sexual pleasure.

She found herself reaching out to touch him back. Sliding her hands through his furry back, grabbing his bottom. Beast slid his tongue up her neck to her ear, and tickled the inside. She squirmed beneath him and moaned. Beauty wanted him. Now. "I want you," she whispered in his ear.

With that, Beast slid himself into her. The sensation of fullness overwhelmed Beauty, and she cried out. "Are you alright?" he asked.

She nodded. "Don't stop," she begged. Beast pushed inside her, first soft, gentle motions, in and out, in and out, and Beauty enjoyed the steadiness of the motion. It was relaxing and exhilarating at the same time. He kissed her neck, sucking and nipping at it, the sensations coupled with him inside her sending her into a tizzy, the waves of pleasure practically overwhelming her. Then, he started to move faster, still steady, but faster and faster, Beauty's pleasure heightening beyond what she'd thought even possible. Her back ground into the mattress, and he grabbed her ass cheeks, while he pressed his hips tighter to her with each thrust. Her ragged breathing increased to keep time with his thrusts, each one building on her enjoyment, each one heightening her closer to climax. Beauty wrapped her legs tighter around him, pulling him deeper into her, enjoying his powerful motions, not sure she could endure such excitement for much longer. Then she came, the waves of the orgasm overwhelming her. She could feel him finish, too, a final long thrust that ended with her feeling his warmth release into her.

Beast kissed her on the mouth, and looked into her eyes. It was as if he was trying to say something but he didn't. He pulled out, and lie next to her, wrapping a furry arm around her and pulling her close to him. "Did you enjoy that?"

Beauty almost laughed. "Of course I did," she giggled. "It was better than anything I could have imagined."

12

Beauty lay in Beast's arms, relishing the afterglow of her experience. She'd never enjoyed anything so much in her life. Beast's arms were warm and cozy. When she first met Beast, she thought his fur would be scratchy and unpleasant in intimate situations, but it was amazingly soft and comforting. She was happy, and it surprised her. She had been so ambivalent when she came to this manor. Coming here was something new, so there was intrigue, but she had also been very worried. Worried that he would be a brute, that she would be made a slave to his sexual whims. But, that didn't seem the case. Yes, they'd only been together this once. Well, once if you counted today. She wondered if she could count the dreams, too. She still wasn't sure what the dreams meant. How the house could cause them to share dreams.

It was odd, though, that Beast didn't know. "How long have you lived here?" she asked him, tracing her fingers over the fur of his chest.

His body tensed beneath hers, and he shifted slightly. "Seven years," he said softly.

"And you've always lived here alone?"

He nodded, and stroked her arm. "Why so many questions, Beauty?"

She looked up at him, his brown eyes looking more than just curious, perhaps a hint of trepidation in them. She smiled reassuringly. "I was just curious," she said, running her fingers around his nipple and tracing it down his belly, past the divot that was certainly his belly button, and resting her hand on his cock. She could feel it start to stiffen, and she grinned at him. She liked having the ability to make him hard, just with her touch. She realized she was

45

losing her train of thought. She'd wanted to know about his life before she came. "You said you'd always lived here alone, so I wondered how long that was. If you'd lived here with your parents and had them show up in a dream like we had the other night, that might have been awkward." She slid her fingers around his cock, then kissed his furry chest.

He grinned back at her. "Yes, very awkward," he said, watching Beauty. She kept her eyes on him as she slowly kissed her way down his torso, his chest first, then his belly down to his waistline until she hovered over his erection, breathing warmly over it, hoping to tease him with the eventual pleasure that would envelop his hard man piece.

His cock was warm and solid, as Beauty slid her hand around its base. She tipped her head downward, sticking out her tongue slightly, and licked the rim of it. Beast moaned in pleasure, and she smiled as she heard it, knowing she was in charge of his pleasure at the moment. She had control. She put just the tip in her mouth, rolling her tongue around it, while her hand traveled to his ball sac. She used her fingertips to gently massage the area, and took more of his huge cock in her mouth. She wouldn't be able to fit the whole thing in — she'd choke to death — but she did her best to get as much as she could. She mimicked the motion of intercourse, in and out, in and out, making sure her mouth was well lubricated. She actually enjoyed the taste of him. His cock was a bit earthy and rugged, just like him. The skin was smooth and supple, and felt so pleasant against her tongue. She heard him grunt with pleasure and picked up the speed of her motion. She wanted him to feel the same type of pleasure he'd given her. So, she rocked with him and teased his testicles with her fingers, and soon he exploded in her mouth. It was salty and sticky, not the most pleasant taste, but she swallowed, figuring that was the most expedient thing to do.

When she was finished, she lifted her head and winked at him. "How was that, big guy?"

"Better than I'd even imagined," he said, mimicking her earlier statement. He grabbed hold of her and pulling her up so her face was level with his. Then he kissed her on the lips. "What can I do for you?"

She shook her head. "Nothing right now. I'm exhausted," she laughed. "Frankly, you've done too much for me today already."

Beast rolled his eyes.

"If you want," he said. "We could go for a walk in the garden, or we could read together. I know you like Ferus Lucunditas. But, there are other books in the library, I'm sure we could enjoy."

Beauty sat up, startling Beast. "Wait, did you say there was a library?"

Beast looked at her, confused. "Yes," he said. "I've seen you reading books. Where have you been getting them, if not the library?"

She frowned. "It's an enchanted house. I've been asking for them, books I've read before, books I'd heard about but never read. Then they'd just appear. I had no idea there was a library."

Beast laughed. "Well, if you've got enough strength left, I'll be glad to show you the library."

13

Beauty was ecstatic to see the library. She loved books, and seeing so many — thousands upon thousands, probably tens of thousands — filled her with joy. The room was at the back of the house and had ceilings that were at least 20 feet high and shelves as tall.

The room smelled lovely, too, of ink, crisp paper and wax. She loved this room. She didn't know how she had missed it. She walked over to a shelf in the far corner, for she recognized those books immediately.

"You found Ferus," Beast said, strolling casually behind her.

Beauty pulled a volume off the shelf. "Yes," she said, examining the leather-bound book in her hand. She looked at the volume number: 17. "I don't think I've read this one."

Beast watched her, the book looking so lovely in her hand. "And how did a sweet girl like yourself happen to come across these books?"

Beauty laughed. "Oddly enough, my tutor brought them to me. Giselle said that the prospect of womanly duties in a marriage might be frightening to me, especially since my mother was dead and I would have no one to explain them to me. She said the books might help me to understand, to anticipate."

Beast reached a furry hand out and brushed a stray auburn hair from Beauty's face. "It certainly did help you. I think it proved quite useful."

Beauty laughed, and thought back to their sex earlier. It had been extraordinary. She blushed and closed her eyes, reliving when he plunged deep inside her for the first time. The shock, at his size, at the sensation, at the ripples of pleasure that passed through her in

48

that moment. She opened her eyes, shook her head. "You're the one who proved quite useful."

He smiled lasciviously, "I do know a thing or two," he said, pulling her toward him. "So, this Giselle, she bought them at a book shop?" he said, wrapping his arms around her and nuzzling at her neck.

Beauty pulled back. "I have no idea," she said, laughing. "Why do you care? How did you come by them?"

Beast shrugged. "They were in the library. But, they seem to be rare editions, and given how Catholic the area is, they don't seem to be something the local minister would encourage young maidens to read or be happy that Giselle was showing them around."

Beauty nodded. "You're right," she said. "I was quite surprised anyone published them. This Ferus Lucunditas can't be popular with the church where he lives. Though, maybe he's a pagan and doesn't care."

Beast frowned. "A pagan?" he asked. "Because he enjoys telling love stories that include all the parts — stories that tell in detail how a man should love a woman, and how she might love him — he must be a pagan?"

Beauty raised an eyebrow. "You're right, but people generally, they just don't talk about it. And it's just that I was frightened to read it when I first got it, when I first saw what it was. Giselle just told me to keep it private, to only read it at home. My father saw the cover a couple of times, but because it's so nondescript, he never really took much notice of it. Thankfully. So, Mr. Lucunditas must be very brave, or it's a nom de plume."

"It is," Beast said, matter of factly. "It's Latin. Ferus means Ferocious, and Lucunditas means Pleasure. It is a book of ferocious pleasure."

Beauty opened her mouth in a little O, a look that turned Beast on, immensely. He could feel the blood flowing to his lower region. He pulled Beauty toward him, and kissed her. His hands found her ass, and cupped her cheeks through the layers of clothing. He wondered why women wore so many layers of clothing — chemises, petticoats, skirts, corsets. It might be easier if she walked around naked. Though, if she walked around naked, they would spend their days doing nothing but what he planned to do with her now.

He ripped the layers of her skirts and petticoats right off her. She pulled back, looked up at him, as if shocked. "Is this you being ferocious?" she asked, licking her lips. He was sure her goal was to turn him on further.

"Yes," he growled lowly. "If that's alright with you."

She took a step back, naked from the waist down. She walked away from him, over toward the sofa in a corner. She sat down with her book as if she intended to read, but it was clear she had no intention of reading. She reclined, lying on her back, popping the book open randomly to a page, then spread her legs so he could see her wonderful pink lips that already appeared to be moist. She asked coyly, "And if I said it wasn't alright?"

Beast came toward her, closing the distance quickly. He looked longingly at her open legs, focusing on the curly auburn hair between them. He touched the area gently with his fingers, feeling the hair that was already moist at the lips of her opening. He breathed heavily and stared at her. "Then I would stop," he said. "If you said it wasn't alright with you, then I wouldn't continue."

Beauty frowned, and began to unbutton her corset. "You, Beast, have a wealth of self-control," she said.

He shook his head. "Not as much as you think, but I make efforts to respect your wishes, even when you're toying with me."

She smiled. "I'm sorry," she said, raising an eyebrow as she slipped the corset off, then pulled the remains of her tattered chemise over her head. "I am not toying with you. I want you to be ferocious with me. I want to feel ferocious pleasure."

"As you wish," he said, then buried his face in her breast, suckling them. He grabbed her derriere harshly, squeezing the buns tightly. Not too tight as to cause pain, but enough grip to be noticed. She moaned, "Oh."

He bent down and placed his face between her legs. He licked the inside of her thigh, and she moaned. Then he grabbed both thighs with his hands and pressed them back further, giving him more room. He slid his tongue into her, licked the side of both lips, and then used his tongue to tickle her sweet spot. He heard her breathe out another, "Oh," and did it again. Her legs tightened around his head, and he slid his tongue down her lips. Then, he darted it inside her, slid it round, and listened to her moan, feeling her body shudder with delight. He kept it up until she grabbed the top of his head and said, "I need you in me."

He withdrew his head from her crotch and gently flipped her over so she was on her knees. She seemed surprised but didn't verbalize any objections. He looked down at her perky ass, the round cheeks so perfect and slightly red from where he'd squeezed them. He rubbed her bum with his palm, then leaned all the way forward, so his face was near hers, and licked her neck, his tongue tracing its way down her back. He slid a finger inside her, the warm moistness immediate and pleasant. He used the lubrication to rub, to rub that little area that so turned her on when he massaged it. He heard her moan, an octave higher than before. The moisture kept coming, and she got louder, so he withdrew his finger and slid in his penis. She gasped and then let out a yelp of pleasure as he pushed further in. He gave a hard thrust, and she said, "Dear God."

"Are you alright?" he asked.

A ragged breath escaped her, followed by, "Yes." She moaned, "Don't stop."

He wasn't sure he could stop if he wanted to. He pushed again, hard, causing her butt cheeks to jiggle. Beauty was on all fours, so he reached underneath and grabbed her breasts and squeezed gently as he thrust harder and faster. With every thrust, Beauty gave a breathy, joyful shriek. He watched the muscles of her back tense and contract with the thrust, and her hair shake, thumping against her neck and back in the same rhythm as his thrusts. He could feel her contracting tighter around his massive cock, could feel her body readying itself to orgasm, to shudder and convulse in pleasure, and he wanted to come with her.

His hairy fingers played with her nipples now, and she moaned louder. He pushed once and then exploded inside her. The release felt good, and he smacked her ass and smiled. "Was that ferocious enough pleasure for you?" he asked as he pulled out of her.

She flipped over, a smile of pure delight on her face. "More than enough," she said, and then he curled up on the sofa with her. He wrapped his arms around her, and soon they both fell asleep.

14

Beauty had lived with the Beast for two months now. They spent a great deal of their time having sex. Beauty was thrilled to explore this side of herself. She liked being with Beast, especially the physical pleasure he offered her, over and over and over again. But, also his company during the day and evenings. He was charming, well-read, and often humorous.

He enjoyed walking the grounds with her and tending to the gardens. They'd often just sit and read to each other. If she'd known then what she knew now, she would not have dreaded coming to live here with Beast at all.

In fact, they were living like a husband and wife. This is partly what bothered her. They had not, in fact, been married. Yet, she was like his wife. Only, Beast insisted that being his wife meant something more than this. It meant her making a choice. But did it? He kept insisting she had a choice, when there really wasn't one. She had to be here with him. That was their bargain, their agreement. Saying she would be his wife would not change things in the least.

They had just had sex, and Beast lay entwined with her, his furry legs tangled with her own. She looked at his monstrously large legs and sighed.

"What's wrong, Beauty?" Beast asked, stroking her arm. "You've been a bit distant lately."

She wasn't sure what to say. That she missed her father. What did it matter? She couldn't leave. That was her promise. But...but what if he changed his mind? Surely he had to understand how difficult it was to leave family behind. He had to have had a family once.

"I've just been thinking," she said. "About you. Wondering what you did with yourself before I came."

Beast looked away, then spoke softly. "I was very lonely before you came."

"Did your family ever come to visit you here?"

"No," he said quickly.

Beauty could tell he didn't want to talk about his family, so maybe this was a bad strategy. If he didn't miss his own family, how could he ever understand her longing to see hers? She smiled at him, leaned toward him and kissed his lips. He seemed to relax a little with that, so she decided to try a different approach. "It's just that you said it was my choice if I wanted to be your wife. Since it is my choice, and my father isn't here to look after my interests, I thought I should find out more about the family I would be marrying into. It might be nice to know whether you all hate each other and never speak, or if you love each other but live too far to be with each other."

He was silent a minute, and Beauty wasn't sure what to think. Then, he said, "You're considering becoming my wife?"

Beauty nodded, though she wasn't sure that was true. She wasn't sure what his distinction meant, since they were bound together — just as if they were husband and wife — so long as he held her to her promise to stay with him forever.

"I don't like to talk about the time before I lived here because I was different. Everything was different, and part of me wishes it to be like that again, but I know it can't be," he said. Beauty had no idea what he meant, but she nodded reassuringly so he would continue. "I used to have a mother, a father, an older brother and a baby sister. When I was 10, my mother died while giving birth to my sister, Odette. My father was a merchant who was away a lot, so my older brother Jacques taught me all he knew about life and women. Only all the stuff Jacques taught me was wrong. I love them all very much, especially little Odette. But I don't see them anymore, because I am here. They do not come visit me because they do not know what has become of me. If we were married, if you loved me truly, it is possible we could go visit them. I think they would like you."

Beauty threaded her tiny fingers through Beasts massive ones, to hold his hand. "Do you miss them?"

His hand squeezed hers tighter. "I don't let myself miss them because that would make me sad. You shouldn't let yourself miss your father either. It's better to just enjoy what the two of us have, right here, right now."

It was not what she wanted to hear. It was, in fact, the exact opposite of what she had been hoping to hear. Beauty lay her head on Beast's chest and tried not to sulk. If she told him she missed her father, he would not care. He would simply tell her to stop it. He truly was a beast, just like his name suggested. And then it hit her, that Beast couldn't be his name. His siblings were named Jacques and Odette.

"What is your name?" she asked.

Beast tensed, and Beauty sat up. "Beast is my name," he said.

She shook her head. "It can't be. A mother who names her children Jacques and Odette would never name a child Beast."

Beast pursed his lips and dragged his fingers through the mane of black fur on his head. "I guess if you are going to make a decision about being my wife, I should tell you the entire truth," he said grimly. "Or as much of it as I can tell you."

Beast sat up, too. Beauty pulled the blanket up to cover herself more, not wanting him distracted by her nakedness. Beast took a deep breath and began. "I didn't always look like this, Beauty," he said. "I used to look like a normal man. I lived with my father, brother and sister. As I said, my father was away often. He traveled to buy goods and make deals. So, that left Jacques and me to our own devices. The nanny, Genevieve, tried to rein us in, but we didn't listen. Genevieve mainly cared for Odette, and sometimes bedded Jacques."

Beauty's mouth opened in mock shock.

Beast grinned. "Don't look so surprised. We were wealthy, and she was poor. She wanted more, hoped for more. There were many girls like that in the village where we lived. Jacques taught me how to trade on a girl's desire for more. He taught me how to imply more but promise nothing, so they would be willing to have sex with me. I was not nice, Beauty."

Beauty sat still beside him, simply listening.

"And then one day, I found a woman who I wanted, who was the crown jewel of attractiveness," he said, getting a far off look in his eyes. He glanced down at Beauty, caught sight of a nipple sticking out from the blanket, and smiled. "Though, in retrospect, she paled in comparison to your Beauty."

Beauty laughed. "You don't have to say that. I understand there were others." Somehow Beauty had known he'd been with other women. That Ferus Lucunditas had not taught him all his skills. That there were others. And hearing about it now made sense.

"I'm not just saying it," Beast said. "It's true. She doesn't compare to you, but, at the time, I was smitten with her, and I wanted her. One evening, I tried to have my way with her; she didn't want to and I …"

His voice trailed off, and Beauty asked, "You took her by force?"

Beast shook his head. "I would have. But, it turns out she was friends with a sorceress. The girl, Isabelle, said words I didn't understand, and then the sorceress appeared. I couldn't see the sorceress' face; it was hidden by a hooded cloak. But, I could see her glowing red eyes beneath. She cursed me, saying I would look as beastly on the outside as I was on the inside. Then she sent me here, saying I must live in this enchanted manor. I am too frightening to be among the public, to be with my family. So, I stay here. It's also safe here," he said softly.

Beauty's eyebrows squished together in confusion. "How could you not be safe?" she asked, staring at his muscular body. His sheer size, coupled with his ferocious claws and fangs, would make him a match for anyone.

"The sorceress knew who I was, that my name carried weight, that even as this hideous creature, some might still try to help me and get in my good favor. So, I was told that I could not be called by my name anymore. I must be known only as Beast. If anyone calls me by the name I was born with, then I shall die."

Beauty's mouth popped open in shock. "Someone saying your name will kill you?"

Beast shook his head. "Not saying it. I'm sure my father or brother have said it since I left, but actually looking at me, this horrific creature that I have become, and calling me by that other name. That will kill me."

Beauty leaned on him, resting her head on his chest. It was a horrific fate — to be afraid of seeing someone you know because that person calling you by your name would lead to your death. No wonder he had no problem staying away from his family. If he told them who he was, he would end up dead. He had been effectively banished, even though that wasn't the sorceress' exact punishment. She understood now why he was so lonely.

Beauty kissed his furry chest. "I'm glad you're not alone anymore,

Beast."

He kissed the top of her head. "I'm glad, too, Beauty. And," he said, his voice sounding slightly choked up. "I sometimes wish you could call me by my name. I imagine how lovely it would sound rolling off your tongue, but I'm glad that you know me at all, by any name. Even if it is Beast."

15

A nother two months passed and Beauty had tried to be happy with Beast. She understood that she was the only person whom he could be with, whom he could talk to. She tried not to resent being here. But it was becoming increasingly harder. She missed her father.

She missed her home. She missed the visits from Giselle and the occasional journeys to town to peruse the shops, even if she hadn't bought anything. It had been nice to sometimes see the hustle and bustle.

Beauty was sitting in the garden, looking at the flowers. She thought it amazing that flowers of pure gold could grow here. The fact that they were pure gold was actually only half the marvel. The other half was the fact that they remained in bloom always, even through the cold winter months that had just passed. Yes, these roses were amazing, Beauty told herself. She was trying to remain caught up in the wonder of the house so that she could forget the sorrows worrying her own heart. Only, it didn't seem to be working.

Beast strolled up beside her, probably having come from cutting firewood. He seemed to like the physicality of the activity, as she supposed the house could have provided as much firewood as was necessary, if only he'd asked.

Though, maybe that's why she enjoyed cooking a pastry in the kitchen sometimes. There were times when the fun was in doing the activity, not the end result.

Beast put a hand on Beauty's shoulder, and she turned and smiled at him. "Cut enough wood?" she asked.

He nodded, then stared at her with a touch of melancholy in his expression. It made her uncomfortable, so she turned to look at the flowers again. "Beauty," he said, so she turned back to him. "Are you happy here?"

She breathed out. If only she knew. Part of her was, but part of her felt like some of her life was missing. Left behind with her trunk, and everything else she was forced to abandon on her hurried departure with Beast. She forced a smile and said, "Yes, I'm happy."

Beast stared at her, as if he wasn't quite sure he believed her. His fur-covered hand reached out and grabbed hers, held it. She enjoyed the sensation. It was never something she would have imagined she'd enjoy, but the softness of his fur, the gentleness of his hand, made her feel warm and happy.

"Beauty," he said. "I know when you arrived here, I said marriage would be your choice. It is your choice, I mean. I just want to know if you would consent to be my wife."

Beauty tried not to look as shocked as she felt. Yes, she knew what he had told her when she arrived, but she hadn't expected him to ask. Not now. Especially not now when she felt so homesick. She shook her head. "I can't," she said simply, pulling her hand from his and walking away. She went inside and upstairs to her room.

A few minutes later, Beast knocked on her door. She bade him come in and he sat next to Beauty on a chaise longue near the window. "Is there something I can do to change your mind, to help you reconsider? I mean, you said you're happy here."

Beauty stared into his brown eyes, his furry, bestial face, remembering once how his fangs and size had frightened her. Only, now she enjoyed seeing his face, enjoyed his company, enjoyed his sexual prowess. "I am happy," she said. "As happy as I can be here, Beast. You've been nothing but kind to me and generous in spirit. And even in telling me I have a choice, there is a certain kindness in that. But, you..." Beauty stopped herself. She couldn't say she felt trapped by him. It would hurt his feelings.

She stood up. "You and I will continue the way we've been." She smiled at him and tried to turn the tables. "Aren't you happy with how we are, how we live?"

He stood up, too. "I may be a beast on the outside, but I have the heart of a man, a heart that yearns for the love of his woman, of her promise to love him and only him forever. So, I am happy to be with you now, but I do desire more."

He'd laid his heart bare for her to see, and for that she was glad, but she could not give him what he wanted in return. "I'm sorry. I can't say yes to you, Beast."

Beast kissed the top of her head. "Very well," he said, then walked out.

16

Beauty and Beast spent the next two weeks living a somewhat strained existence. They still were intimate, but it was clear that Beauty's refusal of Beast's marriage proposal had hurt him.

On this day, Beauty was in the library, looking for something good to read. She saw the line of Ferus Lucunditas books on the shelf. This time, she noticed something about the books she hadn't noticed before. These editions all had the publication year and month. There were three published per year for the last six years, for a total of 18. And this was March and that meant that a new book should be out soon. She wondered if it would simply appear on the shelf and she'd get to see it, or if she actively had to do something to make it appear.

"Give me Volume 19," she said. Then she waited. Nothing happened. She frowned.

She heard a creaking noise and turned to see the door to the library open. It was Beast. "I thought I heard you?" he said.

Beauty nodded. "Yes, I just noticed that the Ferus Lucunditas books are published three per year, in March, August and December. That means we're due another one."

Beast laughed. "And you're excited about that?"

"Well, yes," she admitted. "I have so little to look forward to; let me have this small treasure."

Beast frowned and walked over to her. "So, this is all you have to look forward to?"

Beauty realized her mistake and bit her lip, as she tried to think of how to explain herself. "No, it's not the only thing," she said. "It's just that I'm homesick. I miss my routine, Giselle, and, most of all, my father. You're wonderful to me. It's wonderful here, but sometimes the lack of my usual things bothers me. So, Ferus is like a little taste of home. Like, me getting a book from Giselle, going to my room, reading it by myself and touching myself."

Beast wore a crooked smile. "Do tell," he said. "Did you touch yourself often when you read them?"

Beauty could feel herself blushing. Despite the things she'd done with Beast, she still felt self-conscious talking about intimacies. "I'm sure most people who read that book do that. What is it you did when you read the books?" She raised an eyebrow seductively.

"Would you like me to show you?" he asked, walking toward her. "I'll show you if you show me."

It was an intriguing idea to Beauty. She'd never seen a man touch himself. Her curiosity got the better of her. "Alright," she said. "Show me."

Beast lay down on the sofa, the same one they'd used last time they'd fornicated in this room. He pulled down his britches, exposing his penis, which lay in a heap, still somewhat flaccid. Beauty walked over and sat on the floor beside him. Part of her wanted to grab his penis, touch it, take it in her mouth, make it hard and ready for her. But, this was not what he wanted. He wanted to show her what he did. And she was intrigued to see.

He put his hand on his cock, and it immediately started to come to life. It grew long and hard in seconds, and watching it caused her to moisten down below. Beast wrapped his right hand around it and began to gently, softly, move his hand up and down over the entire length. He got into a rhythm, his hand moving faster and faster, him remaining silent, his eyes closed in concentration. The look on his face was peaceful and dedicated, and Beauty liked it. She liked watching the muscles in his arm flex as he moved his hand, liked watching his erection slide in an out, like a gopher popping out of its hole. The muscles in Beast's legs tightened too, as he performed his ritual. He was quieter when he pleased himself than when he was with her. She wondered if he offered more sound when he was with her, to let her know what pleased him, or if he simply had more pleasure when he was with her than when he was by himself. His mouth parted, and he let out a small gasp of pleasure.

She watched as his hand moved faster and faster. Then, she saw it stop, and the head of his penis spit its gooey, cream-colored mix right onto Beast's belly. It wasn't a single spurt, but three spurts, one after another, and then she looked up to Beast's face, an expression of self-satisfaction resting on his lips. His breathing was steady and heavy.

He opened his eyes and turned toward her. "Did you like that?"

"Yes," she said.

"And you'll show me?"

Beauty nodded. A towel appeared, and Beast cleaned himself. Then, he stood and offered her his spot on the sofa. Beauty had taken to wearing less clothing since it was just her and Beast in the manor. Today, she'd been in her nightgown with a cloak over it to keep her warm. She disrobed quickly and lay on the sofa naked. As she lay there, she felt self-conscious about doing this in front of him. He had done it for her, but he was different from her. He was strong and self-assured with sex. It seemed, with his powerful body and insatiable sex drive, it would be impossible for him to fail at anything sexual.

Beauty enjoyed the physical pleasure, but she didn't have the confidence. So, as Beast stared at her, she lay there, unable to muster the mood necessary to do this in front of him. "It's hard," she said, "to do this with you staring at me."

"Close your eyes," Beast said. "Pretend I'm not here."

Beauty closed her eyes and thought about Beast. She thought about how she longed for him to touch her, how good it would make her feel, and then she began to touch herself in those ways. She slid her fingers around her breasts, down her abdomen and into her tuft of woman hair. Her fingers grazed the outside of her lips, then pushed inside, where it was wet and moist. She started with two fingers, gliding them deep inside her. She opened her mouth, releasing a joyful gasp as she felt the thrill of their immersion. She arched her back as she got into a rhythm and touched her breasts with her other hand, heightening the pleasure. She increased the pace of the thrusts, breathing in time with them and felt the sweet relief of coming.

She opened her eyes to find Beast sitting on the floor next to her, staring intently, a look of desperation on his face. "I want you right now" he whispered.

When she nodded, he stood, and she saw he was completely erect. Within seconds, he mounted her and thrust inside her with reckless abandon. He pounded her and growled as he did so, grabbing her butt cheeks and squeezing. Her hands found his back, and pulled him close to her. She enjoyed the power of his thrusts, the frenzied, uncontrolled passion. She pressed her fingers deep into his back, holding on while he banged her insides. It was unrelenting, and she liked it that way, as he got to a pace she found almost unbearable in its pleasure. Then finally, he released, thrusting hard, with a growl, and then collapsing on top of her. His exhausted breathing matched her own.

He kissed her on the cheek, and then adjusted himself so he lay next to her. She was completely satisfied by that exploit, surprised a little that mutual masturbation could be such a turn on for great sex. She lay there and closed her eyes, with Beast's arms around her. After a few minutes like that, Beast whispered in her ear, "I love you, Beauty."

She lay there stunned, unmoving. She had not wanted him to say that, because he would want her to say it back. And she couldn't. Not when she felt so trapped in this house. She pretended to be asleep.

17

There was a knock at Beauty's bedroom door. It could only be Beast, for no one else was in the house except him. Even so, he always knocked, offering her a chance to deny or welcome his entry. "Come in" she called, as she tied a ribbon around the waist of her chemise like it was a belt.

"I like it when you walk around undressed," Beast said.

Beauty smiled. "Well, it's just you and me, so there's not much point in the corset and petticoats and all that. I figured I'd go with just what I needed."

Beast nodded, and had a look of yearning on his face as he eyed Beauty. She wasn't sure she was up for any more sex, as they'd been at it so much lately. Watching him pleasure himself had been interesting, but pleasuring each other was infinitely more rewarding.

"You came to stare at me in my chemise?" she asked.

He shook his head. "No," he said, then smiled slyly. "I think I have a solution to your problem."

Beauty stared at him quizzically. "And what problem is that?"

"That you want to see your father."

Beauty's mouth opened in shock then she smiled. "You'll let me go see him?" she asked, but he was shaking his head no even before she had finished the question. "Then what?" she asked, feeling betrayed.

"I'll show you," he said, holding out a hand. "Come with me."

Beauty looked at his outstretched palm, and then placed her own hand inside his, with slight hesitation. He had never hurt her before, but she wasn't sure she liked whatever he was going to show her. She wanted to see her father, and if she couldn't leave, she couldn't see him.

Beauty followed Beast out of her room, down a hallway, to a book case with a statue on it. Beast touched the statue, and the wall opened. Beauty stared, shocked. This manor had a secret room. She followed Beast inside a small room with a single chair in it and a mirror on the wall.

"It's enchanted," he said.

"The room?" Beauty asked.

Beast shook his head. "The mirror," he said. "You simply ask it to see anyone you wish and it will show you that person." Beauty was speechless, her mind still not quite believing what she was seeing. She looked at the mirror, wondering if it really could be. "I'll show you," Beast said. He turned to the mirror, and said, "Show me Odette."

Before them on the mirror, a young girl appeared. She was probably 14 or 15, with honey blonde hair and a beautiful smile. The family must have been well off, as she was wearing a fancy dress and expensive-looking jewelry. She was sitting in a room with a woman who appeared to be her tutor.

They watched for a few seconds as the girl wrote something on a piece of paper, but the moment Odette opened her mouth to speak, Beast said, "Stop." The image of the girl went away and the mirror reflected Beauty and Beast in the room. Beast was staring at the floor, his fist clenched. She'd thought it had been a sign of a hard heart that he'd told her to forget about her family, but as she watched his reaction to his sister, she realized she'd been wrong. He'd told her to forget because that's what he wanted — to forget the anguish he felt at missing his family.

She grasped his hand and gave it a squeeze. "That was amazing — that the mirror let you see her," she said softly. Beast nodded. "How do you do it exactly? Do you have to know where the person is to see them?

Beast shook his head. "No, just ask for the person, and it will know where they are and show them to you?"

Beauty nodded. That seemed simple enough. She bit her lower lip and thought. But, she wanted more than just to see her father. "Can the person see you, or just you see the person? Can we talk to the person?"

The Beast hesitated, then said, "It depends." Beauty raised her eyebrows, so Beast continued. "I've found that I have the ability to... project."

"What does that mean?"

"You remember the day the carriage arrived for you, to pick you up?"

Beauty nodded. "Yes, you were there in the carriage, and then you disappeared."

Beast shook his head. "No, I was here, in this room. I was able to project an image of myself there, with you. I put on the cloak to make it seem as if I wanted to stay in the shadows, but I was here in this room. I could see you, and you could see me, as if I were there with you."

Beauty stared at him, trying to remember that day, trying to remember what she saw. Had she actually touched him that day? She didn't think so. And he disappeared as if by magic. But, what if he was never really there? "So, I can ask to see my father, and then project to speak to him?"

Beast nodded. Beauty felt the joy building in her. She could see her father again. She could speak to him. A smile broke across her face, and she could feel it pinching at her ears since it was so large. She wrapped her arms around Beast. "Thank you," she said. "Thank you so much." Then she turned and walked toward the door.

"Beauty," Beast said, confused. "Where are you going?"

She laughed, realizing she must seem a bit crazy. "To put on some clothes. I can't let my father see my like this. He'll think you've been doing exactly what you've been doing with me." She winked at Beast. "We can't have that, now can we?"

* * *

When Beauty returned a few minutes later, her hair fixed in a simple knot in the back and her corset on, she looked radiant. It was happier than Beast had seen her in the past couple of months. He realized now her melancholy was caused by homesickness, and this was sure to be the cure.

Beauty faced the mirror and tentatively said, "Show me my father, please." There, on the face of the glass, was Pierre. Only, he wasn't at his modest cottage in the countryside. He appeared to be in prison. His hands and feet were shackled, and he had a bowl of gruel in front of him. "Father," Beauty said frantically. "Mon Dieu. Papa," she cried out. "Papa, what has happened? What is going on?"

She turned to Beast. "Why can't he hear me?" she asked. "You said I could project."

Beast placed a hand on her shoulder. "You have to concentrate to project. And it's possible that you can't. Maybe it's something only I have the power to do."

"But, why wouldn't I be able to project, Beast?" she asked. "Why just you?"

"Don't worry about why," he said. "Just turn around, close your eyes and concentrate on your father, on trying to get your message across to him." Beauty turned and closed her eyes, he assumed to concentrate. He didn't want to have to answer her questions. He didn't want to have to admit that maybe projecting worked for him because he was bound to this manor. He could never leave it. However, he could send the enchanted carriage, so long as it had a live animal pulling it, to do his bidding.

"It's not working," Beauty said, frustration clear in her voice.

Just then, in the mirror, a man walked up to Pierre. He had brown hair, a chiseled jaw and wore fine clothing. "Monsieur LaVigne," the man said as he bent down toward Pierre. "If you will just bring your daughter from hiding, I will forgive all of this. But, if you do not, you will be executed in two days. You cannot promise me your daughter and, in anticipation of our marriage, have me pay your debts, only to refuse to deliver her."

Pierre coughed, then said in a whisper. "I told you, Monsieur Dumas, I was coming to pay my debt to you."

"Only it was stolen by bandits as you came," Dumas said coldly. "Pierre, is it really worth dying to keep me from my bride?"

"I swear to you, follow the path in the forest, and you'll find the beast's lair. You'll find Beauty there."

"Enough lies," Dumas said. "Jailer, please let me out. I will be back in two days to witness his execution."

The image faded from the mirror, and Beauty turned frantically to Beast. "We have to go back. We have to save him," she said. "We have to explain."

She turned and started toward her room. Beast wasn't sure what to do. He couldn't let her leave. She'd never come back if he let her leave. However, the sole reason she'd come was to save her father. If her father was just going to die anyway, die because Beast had prevented Beauty from being delivered…. The thought of that made him shudder. He went to Beauty's room and found the house had already provided her a traveling bag. She was packing some clothes in it. He felt dread and some other feeling building in him, but he was at a loss to describe what it was. It was unpleasant and weighed him down. It wasn't until she looked up from her packing and saw him standing in the doorway that he realized what the other feeling was: shame. Beauty stopped packing and stared at him. He said nothing, but her face crumpled, and she started shaking her head as she walked toward him.

"Don't say I can't go," she said.

"You promised," he said softly. "You promised to stay here forever."

"To save my father," she said. "But now he is going to die if I don't go. Please," she said, tears streaming from her red-rimmed eyes. "Please, if what we've had has meant anything to you, please let me go."

"I can't," he whispered, but looked away from her.

"You can," she said, falling to her knees, bowing before his feet. "I am begging you, please."

He couldn't help but look at her, watch her beg him, and he felt cruel. He felt like a monster, but if he let her go.... He couldn't let her go. There had to be another solution, something other than her leaving. "I can't let you go," he said.

She sobbed a minute more, with Beast feeling worse with every pained cry, then finally she calmed enough to look up at him. She stood, wiped her eyes, and then spit in his face. "You keep telling me I have a choice," she said venomously. "You are a liar. I have never had a choice. Never. I have been kept here under threat of my father's death, and now it will happen anyway. Well, if you offer me simply the paltry choice of whether to be your wife or not, then no! The answer will always be no. Always. I will never forgive you for this, Beast. Never. I heard you the other day when you said you loved me. Well, I will never love you. Never. By keeping me here, you are as responsible for my father's death as the man who swings the axe."

He stared, unable to respond. Probably because she was right. He kept looking at her, not wanting to leave her, even though she was so angry with him.

"Get out," she said. Beast remained still, too shocked by what was happening to move. When he didn't go, Beauty took both hands and shoved him. "Get out," she said.

He opened his mouth to say something, but there was nothing to say. He turned and left her room.

Beast spent the next two hours thinking. Beauty was right. Nothing here had been her choice, as much as he had tried to present it as such, as much as he tried to make her choose him. She probably continued to refuse to marry him because refusal was the only thing that actually felt like a choice. Everything else had been forced upon her.

He went back upstairs to Beauty's room, his gifts in the bag on his shoulder, hoping to make things right. He didn't knock this one time, because he knew she would send him away. When he opened the door, he found her lying face down on her bed sobbing.

"Beauty," he said softly.

"Go away," she cried out.

"I won't," he said. "But you may. Go away, that is. You may go to your father."

Beauty's sobs stopped, and she sat up and eyed him as if he were a figment of her imagination. She got down from the bed, walked over to him, and asked tentatively, "I may go?"

"Yes," he said. "If you promise to come back."

She nodded. "Yes, of course," she said, taking Beast's hand into both of hers and kissing it. "Yes, I promise. I will come back."

"You'll need these things," he said, using his free arm to tap the shoulder satchel. He walked to Beauty's bed and emptied the contents of the bag onto the mattress. There were several gold roses, a book, and some papers.

"There should be enough gold to pay for your father's debts and give him enough money to live for the next few years," Beast said. "The book is the one you asked about. It's Volume 19. It appeared a few minutes ago. I hope, when reading it, you will think of me. And the papers are what you will need to convince Dumas that you cannot be his. They are papers, signed by your father, agreeing to our marriage, which was sanctified when he left you last November."

Beauty stared up at the Beast, bit her lip. "I thought you said we would only be married if I agreed."

"That's true," Beast said. "We are not married. The papers are a forgery, as your father didn't really sign them. But if you don't have them, I fear Dumas will be able to claim you as his own. It will not be a lie if you tell him we have consummated the relationship."

Beauty stared at the paper. She picked it up and read the contract: "Angelina 'Beauty' LaVigne is married to Emile de Verran." She looked up at Beast. "Who is," she started, but he clamped his hand over her mouth.

"I have given you a secret that can kill me," he said softly, looking deeply into her eyes, hoping this act showed her exactly how much he loved her. "Please don't say my name here."

When he removed his palm from her mouth, it was still open. She closed it for a second, and then said. "Beast, you shouldn't have. The sorceress said it would kill you if I called you this." Her eyes were starting to fill with tears again. "What if I make a mistake?"

"I trust you," he said, taking a hand and wiping away her tears. "I trust you to come back and I trust you not to hurt me."

Beauty stared, as if amazed. She bit her lip and frowned with worry. "What if someone I show it to calls you by your name?"

"No one can find this place. The enchantment prevents someone looking for it from finding it. I get the occasional straggler, like your father, but no one who comes looking for this place finds it. You don't have to worry about that. Tell your father you made up the certificate and used the name of a long-lost count you heard about. No one will find me here. The carriage is enchanted and can always find its way back when saddled to a horse. Take the carriage to your father. If you go now, you might be able to make it before the last judge goes home. You may be able to get your father out tonight and settle him back at home. Stay with him a few days and then come back to me. The carriage will bring you back."

Beauty hugged Beast, kissed him on the lips, a long, lingering kiss, grabbed the bags and headed to the door.

18

Beauty had been too wound up to do anything on the carriage ride but look out the window, searching for the familiar territory that was home. When she got to her father's house, she found it boarded up, as she'd suspected, so she had the carriage take her straight to the jail. She had the gold and could pay her father's debts.

Not sure how she could explain a driverless carriage — a horse that simply knew where to go because she commanded it — she had the carriage park a few blocks down, and walked the rest of the way. She'd left the Ferus Lucunditas book in the carriage, along with the bag of clothes she had packed and half of the gold roses. But she brought the satchel with her fake marriage certificate and five gold roses.

It was already dark outside now. This was good and bad. It meant her carriage without a driver at the reins was less likely to be noticed. But, it also meant the jailer might put her off until tomorrow. The value of the five roses she carried with her was more than double her father's debt.

She passed a few people on the street, but not many. She was the only woman, and she began to wonder if it was a good idea to be out at this time of night. She sighed. It didn't matter. She had to get her father.

She arrived at the jailer's door and banged. There was silence, at first, and then someone came to the door, opened it a crack. It was Monsieur Rocharte, the jailer. "Beauty?" he said.

"Yes," Beauty answered. "Let me in. I've come to get my father."

M. Rocharte opened it further, allowing Beauty to enter. "Dear, your father can't get out. He owes a great sum in debt. He is to be executed in two days. He also violated a contract for your betrothal."

"He never signed a contract with M. Dumas," Beauty said. "It was a verbal agreement. He changed his mind. However, he did sign a contract with my husband."

M. Rocharte's eyes widened. "Your husband?"

"Yes," Beauty replied. "I am married. The beast was a representative of my husband, and my father signed a contract for my marriage."

M. Rocharte shook his head. "It doesn't matter, Beauty. He's already been sentenced. I can't do anything. Only a judge can."

Beauty reached into her satchel with both hands and pulled out a golden rose. "This is a gift," she said, holding the flower out toward him. "It's from my husband and myself to you. It's to show our appreciation for your taking the time to bring a judge from his home so he can re-adjudicate the case with my new evidence. I have my marriage contract, as well as the payment for my father's debts."

M. Rocharte looked greedily at the rose and attempted to gingerly pick it up. Only it was too heavy. Astonishment, then pure avarice, filled his face. He took both hands, lifted the rose, and said to Beauty, "Lock the door when I leave, and do not open it until I come back." She nodded and watched him leave in the night.

* * *

The power of gold still somewhat shocked and amazed Beauty. The judge convened court after hours, looked at Beauty's marriage agreement, and took the gold flowers she had in repayment of the debt for M. Dumas. After receiving an extra gold flower for his own time and inconvenience, the judge ruled in favor of Pierre and ordered him released.

Beauty struggled with a weak Pierre to the carriage, which took them back home. In the carriage, she found an iron bar, which was just what she needed to pry loose the boarded door. She wondered briefly if the carriage were enchanted in the same way as the house — the thing she needed would be there. But, she didn't have time to find out. She needed to get her father inside. He was shivering and gaunt.

Once she got them inside, she lit the fire, because it was freezing inside and her father seemed so cold. He'd been pudgy when she left him, but now he was all skin and bones. No telling what they had been feeding him. Probably bread crumbs and water. No vegetables, fruits, cheeses or meats, probably. She looked in the cupboards, but they were bare. Her father had been in that jail for months, and whatever had been in the home was gone. Perhaps it had been taken when they'd boarded it.

She went out back to the vegetable garden, to see if something, anything, had started to sprout again, but when she got there, it was just a pile of dead vines. It was still too cold. Maybe in a couple of weeks there would be something. She went in and looked at the rooms. Everything was gone. Everything. They had taken it all to pay her father's debt to Dumas, and still they'd put him in prison. Still they'd planned to execute him. She needed to do something

She ran back out to the carriage and sat inside it. She closed her eyes and thought of a warm feather mattress wound into a roll. She opened her eyes, and there it was. She said a quick prayer of thanks that the carriage was as enchanted as the manor. Then, Beauty lugged the mattress inside and lay it on the floor a few feet from the fire. She told her father to lie on it, which he did, moving slowly as if the actions caused his bones to ache. She ran back to the carriage, conjured blankets and came back and covered her father. She spent the evening using the enchanted carriage to get the supplies her father and she would need to live for the next few weeks. Clothing, food, pots, pans, another mattress, firewood, seeds for the vegetable garden, more blankets, even a couple of chairs and a small table to eat at.

She had been thankful for the cover of darkness and the cottage's secluded location. No one saw the magic that had come from the carriage. While she could have packed some of the things, there was no way all that she brought out of the carriage could have fit inside it.

Beauty was exhausted and went to sleep in her old room. She woke early in the morning to her father's moans. She made him vegetable soup and gave him some bread. He ate that alright and went back to sleep.

He'd barely been awake during the hearing last night. He'd simply nodded when the judge asked if he'd signed the contract. Pierre was generally an honest man, but even he knew lying about that matter was best. Or perhaps he had been so out of it that he would have said yes to anything he thought would grant him freedom.

Beauty spent the next day nursing her father and trying to get the house in order for when she left again. Part of her wanted to take her father with her, to have him live in the enchanted manor with her and Beast. But she was afraid. Beast's greatest gift to her, that phony marriage certificate, had exposed his real name. She'd told her father that the certificate was fake, that it was created to help her get out of this situation. But she worried that he might figure it out at some point. That he might call Beast Emile, and then, then…. The very thought of what would happen hurt her heart. She couldn't take that chance. She would have to nurse her father back to health and get him prepared for life without her. She would go back to Beast and tell him she loved him. She would agree to be his wife.

But she needed her father safe and healthy first.

There was a knock on the door. Beauty went to answer it. When she opened it, she recognized the man immediately: M. Dumas. He was dressed in a fine suit, with a top hat hiding much of his sandy brown hair. His face was freckled, and he smiled crookedly at her. She had the urge to slam the door in his face.

"I'm Mathieu Dumas," he said, tipping his hat. "May I come in, Mademoiselle?"

Beauty shook her head. "It's Madame," she corrected. "I am married, and I am sure my husband would not have the man who sought to steal me from him and imprison my father enter this home."

Dumas' smile faded, and his nostrils flared. "So, you still want me to believe that you have married someone else?"

"I have," Beauty said. "And my husband sent gold to repay my father's debt to you. The judge should have given it to you. Though, I must admit, given that you paid my father's creditors, I was surprised to find the house empty when we returned the other day. I had to send my footman to bring us supplies."

Dumas scowled. "So, where is this husband of yours, Monsieur de Verran?"

Beauty smiled and said the exact lie she'd told the magistrate during her father's hearing. "He is a merchant and was due to meet his ship at port, just as we got word of my father's imprisonment. He had our carriage packed and asked our footman to safely guide me home and collect my father. He will join us as soon as he can."

"And your footman?" Dumas asked.

"He went into town to get provisions."

"But he left the carriage and the horse?" Dumas asked, pointing to the horse tied to a post and the nearby carriage.

"There were two horses," Beauty said. "He took one. Good day, M. Dumas." She shut the door and locked it. Breathed out. She was now gladder than ever that her father had stumbled onto Beast's manor. She could not imagine being married to that man. He was cruel and heartless. He would never have been gentle with her, not the way Beast was. He never would have read with her, laughed with her, listened to her.

She was glad to be rid of him.

* * *

Beauty spent the next weeks getting the place back into shape, tilling the garden, planting it, and nursing her father back to health. Pierre no longer woke up whimpering in the night, and he no longer had saggy folds of skin to indicate his impoverished waistline. He was getting healthier, and Beauty was glad of it.

She was sad, though. She had not seen Beast. She had expected him to look in on them, to project to her. She'd even tried talking to him at night, once her father was asleep. She had hoped that he would use his mirror to see her. She always apologized for taking so long and promised she would come back as soon as her father was in good health and he could take care of himself.

She thought that the time to go back to Beast had almost come, even though it was beyond the few days she had promised him.

That night, she made her father pheasant. She said she'd caught it out back, but it had really come from the carriage. She'd basted it well and made her father's favorite sides of yams, braised beans and croissants.

"Father," she said. "I just wanted to let you know that I have to go soon. I have to go back to Beast."

Her father looked up from his plate, a mix of shock and sorrow on his face. "Beauty, no. It's too soon. And that creature," he shivered as he spoke. "He was so ghastly."

Beauty shook her head. "Father, I made a promise to him. He let me leave to come help you, but I promised I would go back. I will keep my promise to him, whether I want to or not."

"Beauty," her father said. "You shouldn't go to this creature if you don't want to. What about your husband?"

"Father, I told you that was all a lie. Beast created it for me, using the name of a count or duke or some such who disappeared years ago. I must go back with him. He's not unkind to me, father."

"Do you want to go?" her father asked.

Beauty paused, not sure what to say. Did she want to go back to Beast? Unequivocally, the answer was yes. But did she want to leave her father? No, she didn't want that. And that really seemed to be what he was asking. "No, father," she said. "I don't want to leave you to go to him. But, I must." She paused, thought a minute. "I would love to have you both in my life. He's really not bad, father. He isn't."

"He just demands that you stay with him."

She shook her head. "That's just it," she said. "He let me go, because he trusted me. He trusted me in a way that I can't really explain to you, Papa, but it means a lot to me. And I can't let him down. I don't want to let him down."

Her father looked quizzically at her. "So you do want to go back?"

She sighed. "I want to see him, but I don't want to leave you."

Her father nodded. "No, it's alright," he said. "All daughters must grow up and move on."

Beauty nodded.

"Are the two of you married?" he asked her.

Beauty shook her head. "He always said I had a choice. He asked me to marry him, and I told him no. He never hurt me because I refused him. He's only been good to me and, truthfully, I miss his kindness."

Her father nodded. "I guess I knew you would go back to him," her father said, then took a bite of his pheasant. "He wrote all those books that you love."

Beauty stopped and stared at her father. "What?"

"Your Beast. His name is Ferus, right? He wrote the books."

Beauty shook her head, still baffled by what her father was saying.

Pierre saw her confusion and started to explain. "I was looking for you earlier. Little did I know you were out hunting pheasant," he said chuckling. "I went in your room and on top of your bag was one of the books. The one with the rose imprint and the name Ferus Lucunditas. I opened it, because it looked newer, and the dedication on the first page of the book was to you. It was signed, 'Beast.'"

Beauty felt pure shock. She hadn't read the book, even though he'd specifically said she should read it. She'd thought about opening it many times, but decided she wanted to read it with him. She'd been toying with reading it last night, but decided against it, thinking that reading it would make her miss him more. She'd just set it on her bag. Her father was staring at her, she realized. She wondered if all the color had drained from her face. That's what it felt like. "Did you read the book, Father?" she asked, choking out the words.

Pierre shook his head. "I wanted to, but the book snapped shut, on its own." He shuddered at the memory. "I figured it was one of his enchanted books, one that knew I wasn't the owner and decided to shut me out."

Beauty nodded. "Excuse me father," she said, getting up and rushing to her room. She picked up the book and opened it to the dedication page. She hadn't remembered any of Ferus' books being dedicated before. But this one was. Right there, typeset, just like the rest of the book. It said:

To Beauty.

My love for you endures. Please enjoy this tale as you care for your father. Then, hurry home to me.

Beast

19

Beast was despondent. He'd not been able to watch another second. He'd refrained from spying on Beauty, from not trusting her, from not taking her at her word. He'd seen how sick Pierre had been. Of course it would take longer than a few days to nurse him back to health.

But, it had been three weeks, and he was at his wits' end. He should at least check to make sure they were alright. And then he'd seen them in the mirror. Beauty was radiant as always and they were having pheasant. She was telling her father she was leaving. That made Beast's heart ecstatic.

But only for a second, because then she had said she was returning only because she made a promise. She would keep her word whether she wanted to or not. When her father had asked if she wanted to go back, she'd said, "No." It was like a dagger to his heart. He'd heard enough of their conversation and cried out, "Stop," to the mirror. He couldn't watch another second. He'd felt so sure that letting her go was the right thing, that he was doing what you did with someone you loved. He thought that you let them take care of the things they needed. He thought that you helped them because you knew they would do the same for you.

He loved her, but it was clear that she didn't love him. He was just her captor, still. After everything, he was still just her captor.

20

Beauty was shocked. It had been a long time since she had been shocked. But this had shocked her. The book, Volume 19, was her and Beast's story. Only it started at the beginning. Before Beast had met her. There was an old woman who cursed him for trying to take the girl, Isabelle. She bound him to an enchanted manor, promising him death if he ever left the grounds. In Ferus' book, there was no way to break the curse. Only, the old woman had said Beast could be happy if he found someone who loved him. The sorceress would not prevent him from being happy if he could find someone who would love a beast.

So Beast spent his first year in the enchanted castle sulking. But the next year, he decided to change, to devote himself to figuring out how to love. He wrote a story on parchment. A story that included detailed love scenes, but that was ultimately about a man finding a woman who would love him, flawed as he might be. The sex was there, but the story, the story was Beast pouring his heart out, hoping to be loved. And when he finished writing on the parchment, he signed it, on a whim, Ferus Lucunditas.

Shortly thereafter, the parchment with his story on it disappeared, and right before his eyes appeared a book, with a rose on the cover. It was a rose just like the ones that grew in his garden. A rose of golden color, but imprinted on the leather. And beneath the rose was Ferus Lucunditas, Volume 1. His story was there, bound and typeset, as if by magic. So, he read it over and marveled at the magic of the manor. Then he thought more and wrote another story over the next few months. When he finished the tale, it appeared there on his shelf again. Volume II.

He did this for six years. From that point on, Beauty recognized the story. She saw her father's visit from Beast's perspective. Beast was so angry with Pierre for stealing that he intended to teach the thief a lesson. Beast remembered the fear he'd felt with the sorceress and knew that fear of death often showed the true colors of a man. He wanted to see what type of man Pierre really was, so he threatened to kill him, dragging him out to the chopping block where he cut firewood. "I marveled at his selfishness," Beast had written, "In offering up an innocent girl to pay his debts, first to a stranger, and then to me. Though he hadn't really offered her to me. He was just telling me to explain. Still, I wanted her, so I decided I would take her. Or perhaps save her, for the man she had been promised to was as awful as I had once been. I made Pierre swear he would give her to me instead. I felt both hopeful, yet reviled, by what I'd done."

Beauty read that passage again and again, and she read others. She saw their relationship from his point of view. His desire to give her a choice in everything that happened at the manor. His desire, his longing, to make her happy. This volume left out the part about his name being deadly, and left out a few of their squabbles, but it relived in detail their sexcapades. Beauty found herself longing for Beast, even more than she had before.

This book, Ferus Lucunditas' Volume 19, ended with Beauty returning and agreeing to be his wife. She closed the book. She wanted her and Beast's real story to end the same way this book did — in marriage. She would return to the manor in the morning. She would apologize again for being so late. She knew he had to have seen her in the mirror, seen her apologizing. He was probably sullen that she hadn't mentioned the book. That was probably why he hadn't projected. She would thank him for it when she saw him tomorrow. She smiled to herself.

There was a loud banging at the front door. Beauty sat up on her feather mattress and tilted her head toward her bedroom door, so she could hear.

She heard the old front door creak open. "Monsieur Dumas," her father said. "You are not welcome here."

"And you are a liar," Dumas said. "I had my men look into Emile de Verran. He disappeared seven years ago. He's presumed dead. He is not married to your daughter. You are a liar, and you will pay for it with your life."

Beauty ran to her bedroom door and opened it just in time to see

Dumas draw his sword and point it at her father.

"Nooo," Beauty screamed. "Don't kill him."

Dumas looked at Pierre, cowered before the sword. Dumas raised the sword and hit Pierre on the head with the hilt. Beauty gasped as her father crumpled to the floor. Dumas looked up at Beauty, satisfaction on his face. "I didn't kill him, but I expect your cooperation for my unexpected kindness. I want to finally see what's under your pretty dress."

Beauty's eyes widened as she realized what he meant to do to her. She pushed her bedroom door shut and tried to hold it that way. She wished the door locked. There was so little furniture in the house, there was nothing to even barricade the door with. "Beast," she called out in her mind. "Please. Please help me."

21

Beast wasn't sure why he returned to the mirror. He supposed he wanted one final look at her. He planned to walk out of the manor tonight, off the grounds, and take his punishment: death. Living without her was too painful. Living with her because she was forced to be there was too painful. It's why he had let her go.

But, he wanted one last look. "Show me Beauty."

Before him on the mirror, he saw her, leaning forward, both hands pressed against her bedroom door, feet planted firmly on the ground, as if trying to keep someone out. Then she toppled backwards, falling onto the floor as the door burst open. It was Dumas. He was walking toward her, and she was shaking her head.

"No, please don't do this," she cried out. "Please, I swear to you I am married."

"You are not married to Emile de Verran. That is a lie."

She nodded. "I'm not married to him," she said. "I am married to Beast." Beast was so shocked by what she said, he could do nothing but watch. "He is the beast my father left me with. He loves me, and I love him. He is kind to me. But, he is cruel to anyone who would try to hurt me. He will kill you if he finds out you're doing this. Just go. Go now, and you'll be safe."

Dumas cackled. "You expect me to believe that? Superstitions and sorcery. There is no beast, just like there is no de Verran. There is only the supple virgin I was promised, who I now plan to take."

He walked toward her, and Beauty scooted backwards across the floor, putting distance between them. "I'm not a virgin," she said. "We've consummated our relationship."

Dumas smiled again. "You'll say anything, won't you?" He shook his head, stepping closer and then kneeled in front of her. "Am I really so bad?"

Beauty was perfectly still. She did not respond to his question. A wise move, Beast realized. She looked into Dumas' eyes, fear in her own and said, "Please don't do this to me."

"Don't worry," he said, grabbing the hem of her dress and shoving it up, "You'll enjoy this."

Beauty began to kick. Dumas pushed her legs down and slapped her across the face, the sound reverberating so loudly that Beast thought he could feel her anguish. Beauty winced in pain and looked back at Dumas, her face filled with fear.

The cad smiled and spoke sternly. "You will stop fighting, or I will hit you hard, like I hit your father, and then I'll do what I want. I'd prefer to hear your moans of excitement, but I'll gladly leave you knocked out with a knot on your head. Do you understand?"

Beauty nodded. Beast had to do something. He couldn't just watch. He closed his eyes, puffed his chest, tried to look menacing and projected. Dumas was unstrapping his pants when Beast growled, "Let her go."

Dumas turned and shrunk back when he saw Beast. The projection was working, Beast thought. "Beauty," he said to her. "Move away from him. This is like our first carriage ride together, so time is of the essence."

Dumas looked at Beast, confused, then at Beauty, who stood and stepped away from Dumas. She walked toward the corner, where she stopped next to a window.

"Look at me," Beast said to Dumas. "The man turned. She is my wife, and if you ever touch her again, I will kill you. Do you understand?"

Dumas nodded. Beast stared at him, growled, and tried to appear menacing. He hoped to give Beauty the time she needed. He watched her slip out the window. She just needed time to get to the carriage, and it would bring her back to the house. Claude was a fast horse, even when pulling the carriage.

"What are you going to do to me?" Dumas asked in a whimper.

Beast snarled and said, "I'm still deciding."

"Please," Dumas said, drawing nearer to Beast, getting down on one knee, "Please don't hurt me."

Beast looked at Dumas and wondered how any man could be so cruel to a woman yet such a coward when faced with someone his equal or stronger. He was so caught up with this thought, with projecting, with making sure Beauty was getting away safely that he didn't notice Dumas draw his sword until it was too late. The sword sliced right through the Beast's projection, dissipating it. Now Beast was staring at Dumas in the mirror, and Dumas was staring at where his sword had swung through the air. Beast was gone from the room, and Dumas appeared confused.

At that moment, one of Dumas' servants ran through the open door into Beauty's room. "I know you asked not to be disturbed, Master," the servant said, panting. "But a carriage just left."

Dumas sneered. "Take some things. Make it look like a robbery, then go home. I will go after the girl."

Dumas ran out of the house, mounted his horse, and rode off after Beauty.

"Show me Beauty again," Beast said to the mirror.

He saw Beauty in the carriage, her chest heaving up and down. There was relief on her face, but fear, too. He could tell she needed him. He projected himself again. "Beast," she said. "Thank God. Thank you for doing that. I couldn't have gotten away without you."

He wanted to touch her, to hold her, to reassure her. But he couldn't. He had to tell her the truth. "You haven't gotten away yet," he said. She looked alarmed. "He's gotten on his horse. He's chasing you."

She shook her head. "No, he can't," she whimpered. "Please, you can't let him get me."

Beast nodded. "You're in the carriage. Use what is there to your advantage, and conjure what you need — a weapon, or something to protect yourself. The carriage is bringing you home. Its enchantment will protect you until you arrive. Once you get here, I can protect you."

"If I don't get home?" she asked, the panic in her voice causing the words to run together. "If he catches up with me?"

"Stay in the carriage. You'll be protected inside the carriage."

Beauty nodded.

"It is hard for me to project and monitor what he's doing. Is it alright if I leave you now to watch what he's doing? I'll be back as soon as you're close to home, to let you know."

She didn't look like it was alright for him to leave her, but she said, "Yes," swallowing hard, rubbing her hands on the skirt of her gown. "Go watch him."

Back in the room with the magic mirror, Beast watched as Dumas pursued Beauty's carriage, getting closer and closer. He knew the carriage wouldn't stop, so Dumas would have to climb on top while it was moving in order to get to Beauty.

Beast saw Dumas take out a small crossbow and aim it toward the carriage. It looked as if he might be trying to shoot the undercarriage, to somehow dislodge a wheel. It would take an expert marksman to make the adjustments at night at that speed. It was a stupid shot, but Dumas seemed intent on it. Beast watched as Dumas' horse got closer to the rear of the carriage. He took aim, but didn't fire, instead sliding the crossbow back to his side. Apparently, Dumas didn't think he could hit that spot either. He whipped the reins on his horse, urging it faster, so that Dumas was now even with the front wheels of the carriage. A shot to the front wheels seemed no easier, so Beast wondered why Dumas was going to attempt that instead of the rear. That's when he saw Dumas point his crossbow and realized the wheels were not the target. "Claude," Beast shouted as the arrow hit the horse pulling the carriage. The animal twitched violently and fell down. The carriage jerked and slid along, the forward momentum carrying both injured horse and its' tow forward.

They weren't going to make it onto the grounds of the manor, and the enchantment on the carriage was coupled with the live horse pulling it. The carriage wouldn't move without Claude. Beast wasn't even sure the carriage door would remain locked.

They weren't that far away, though. Many times, Beast had seen that area when he looked out the window of the top floor. It couldn't be more than five minutes from the manor. He could reach Beauty in five minutes. But, would he make it that long? Would he live that long? Leaving the manor meant death.

"Sorceress," he said aloud. "You put me here for what I did, and you were right to do so, but I beg you that you let me save Beauty from the same fate I had intended for Isabelle so many years ago. Please let me save her before I die for disobeying you."

With that, Beast, for the first time in seven years, fled the manor.

22

The carriage had lurched forward, tilting to one side, then skidded and stopped, but Beauty wasn't sure why. Beast was not there, welcoming her to the manor. But, Dumas didn't seem to be there either. He wasn't banging on the carriage door or trying to pry her out of it.

She wasn't sure what to do. She opened the carriage blinds and looked out. She recognized the area. They weren't far from the manor, but they weren't there, either. She wondered why Claude had stopped. She wondered where Dumas was. She sat still and waited. One minute. Then another. Nothing. She opened the carriage door and looked around. She saw no one. Not Beast, not Dumas. She got out, and when she went to the front, she saw the horse, Claude, on the ground, blood gushing from his skull.

"Claude," she cried out as she looked at him. She started toward the horse, but just then she felt an arm around her waist.

"Got you," Dumas said, triumphant. "I knew you'd get out, eventually." He looked around at the dark sky, "But actually I'd like some privacy for this," he smirked. "Let's go back in."

As Dumas pulled Beauty toward the carriage, she made it hard for him, struggling against him, trying to lower herself to the ground so she was all dead weight. They were battling when she heard Beast's voice. "Let her go," he growled. Dumas turned, so Beauty was forced to turn with him. Dumas laughed. "You again. I thought I vanquished you once. It was easy enough that I'll do it again."

He tossed Beauty to the side, drew his sword and ran toward Beast. Beauty landed with a thud on the ground, but was determined to get up quickly, so she could run toward the manor. Once Dumas discovered Beast was merely a projection again, he would chase her.

She was standing up when Dumas reached Beast. This time, Beast grabbed Dumas sword and broke it in half. Dumas stopped in shock.

So did Beauty. This wasn't possible. He couldn't leave the grounds of the enchanted manor or he would die. He'd said so in the book, in *Volume 19*. Perhaps that part hadn't been true, but that was the one part of their story that made sense, the reason he wouldn't let her leave, because he couldn't follow her. But here he was — outside the manor. She walked toward the two men, her eyes wide as she watched Beast attack Dumas. Beast lifted Dumas in the air with his right hand and used the other to punch him in the stomach. Dumas let out a whoosh, like he'd had the wind knocked out of him, and then he whimpered. Beast growled, then lifted Dumas to his horse, and said, "Never come back here."

Beast smacked the horse on the bum, and it sped off, carrying Dumas on its back. Just as the horse strode out of view, Beast plopped down on the ground. Beauty ran over to him, threw her arms around him. "Beast, oh thank God you came."

Beast's breathing was heavy, startling her. Yes, he'd been in a fight, but it had seemed one-sided and rather short. She had never seen Beast look this exerted, even after chopping firewood. She let go of him to look at him. He looked weak and sick and lay down in the grass, breathing laboriously still.

"Beast," she cried. "What's wrong?"

"I left the manor," he said. "I am dying."

Beauty shook her head, grabbed hold of his shoulder and tried to get him to sit up. "No, you'll be OK. You just have to get back. I'll help you," she said. She gripped his arm and tried to pull him up to a sitting position, but he was so heavy, nothing happened.

"I am dying, Beauty," he said. "I left, but the sorceress, I think she allowed me to live long enough to save you, and for that I'm grateful."

"No, Beast," she cried. He was wrong. He wasn't that far from the manor. He'd lived long enough to get to her. He had to be able to live long enough to get back. He had to. "You can't die," she said. "I came back to tell you that I love you, that I want to marry you."

He smiled at her. "It's kind of you to lie now. But, I heard what you told your father. You were coming back as a promise."

Horror filled Beauty's heart. He'd heard that. "Didn't you hear the rest?"

Beast whispered, "No."

"I just didn't want my father to think I wanted to leave him, but I do want to be with you. When my father told me about the inscription in the book, I went and read it. I read everything. I saw all the love you've shown for me. I love you, Beast. Please," she lay her head on his chest. "Please don't die."

He coughed, then gasped for air. Beauty lifted her head from his chest and scooped one of his hands into hers. "Please, please, please, Beast, stay with me."

"Don't call me," he whispered, and Beauty realized that it was hard for him to speak, that the air wasn't coming to him as it should. She felt the tears stream down her cheeks. Just as she had realized that it was him she wanted all along, he was dying. "Not Beast," he said in gasps. "Call me by my name."

Beauty shook her head. "I can't. That will kill you."

"I know, but I want to hear you say it. I sometimes dreamed of you saying it to me. I want to hear you say it just this once."

Beauty was still shaking her head, but she could see the light fading from his eyes. She could see he was going. He was going to die, and he had only one wish. She had to grant it. "I love you, Emile."

23

Beast was on the ground unmoving, and Beauty lay on his chest, sobbing. She couldn't believe it. He was gone. Gone. To save her. She cried harder, her tears rolling onto his chest. Then, she heard something. Something she hadn't expected. She pressed her ear closer to his chest. Was it? Could it be?

A heartbeat.

She sat up, wiped her eyes, and looked at Beast. The hair on his face, his arms, and his fingers was slowly receding, his body, so massive before, was shrinking, and his snout-like mouth was morphing into a normal man's mouth.

He was becoming a man again. Beauty watched the transformation. She watched the beast she had come to love morph into a man, a man with a slender nose, fine red lips and a mane of thick, curly black hair. His arms and chest were still muscular and toned, but not as broad and bulky as when he was a beast. He still had hair on his chest, only you could see the pale flesh beneath it now. She stared, dumbstruck.

He opened his eyes. "Beauty?" he said, blinking.

"Beast?" she asked.

He nodded, and started to sit up, putting his hand on her leg as he did so. Then he stopped, his eyes widening as he saw his hand. He lifted it closer to his face and examined it. He lifted his other hand and examined it, too. Then he looked down at his feet. He reached up and touched his face. "I'm normal again," he said, amazement in his voice. He pulled her to him. "I'm normal. You broke the curse, Beauty."

She felt his arms around her and they were familiar and strange all at once. It was odd to be here with Beast, and have him be so different. He released her and looked at her. "Beauty," he said. "It's me. I know I look different, but it's me, Emile."

She stared, still feeling awed by the change. Even though he looked different, she wouldn't call him that. "Beast," she said. "I won't say that again. I don't know that it won't kill you, or maybe it did kill you, but I can't risk it again. I won't say it."

He smiled, then leaned in and kissed her. His lips were soft and warm, and the way his tongue moved in her mouth was familiar. It was him, she was sure, but she wasn't used to the new him. His lips lingered on hers a little longer than necessary, leaving them warm on this cool evening. Beast looked around.

"We should go inside, in case he comes back," Beast said, standing. He seemed well now, no signs of the deathly fatigue that had plagued him just moments ago while in his beastly form. "I felt comfortable taking him on without a weapon before. But, I'm not as strong as I used to be."

He took Beauty's hand, and they walked briskly toward the manor, shutting the gate behind them. Once inside, Beauty followed Beast, watching him closely. As a man, he was handsome, with symmetrical features anyone would find attractive. And she found that she did. Not quite in the same way she found Beast attractive when he was furry, but still, there was something there. They walked into the main room and sat down. There was no fire now. Beauty wished there was a fire. Suddenly wood appeared in the hearth, and a fire blazed from it.

"The house is still enchanted," Beauty said, staring at the fire, enjoying its warmth.

He looked at the fireplace, furrowed his brow. "You've broken the enchantment on me, but not on the house, it appears."

"But how?" she said. "How did you become a man again?"

"You read my story?" he asked, then paused. "Our story?"

Beauty nodded.

"I didn't put it all in the book. I knew you were going to read it, so I didn't put it all in. The sorceress told me how to break the spell. She said I had to find a maiden who truly loved me. And you do. That's probably why it was OK for you to say my name, because you said you loved me first, and that broke the curse. Now, I'm free," he said, breaking into a grin. "We are free. We are not bound here."

At that moment, they heard the front door creak open. Beast

stood and grabbed a poker from the fireplace, prepared to fight. Beauty stood behind him, fearful M. Dumas had returned for her. They were both shocked when a woman in a red cloak entered. They could see nothing of her face, only her glowing red eyes.

Beauty heard the poker clatter to the floor, then saw Beast drop to his knees. "Please," he said. "The curse is broken. Please do not punish me again."

A voice floated out from the sorceress. "I am not here to punish you," she said. "You asked for mercy those seven years ago, and I gave it to you. I find those who ask for mercy actually need it most. I simply came to tell you I am proud of your change, and that you may stay here in this manor. You may also contact your family and use your name again. You have changed and repented, which is all that I wanted."

The sorceress turned her attention to Beauty, her glowing eyes focusing in on the girl. Beauty shrank back a little, not quite happy for the scrutiny. "And Beauty," the sorceress said. "My sister Giselle was right. You are a very special girl. When Beast first began writing his stories, I thought he had learned nothing, and simply missed his debauchery. But, I showed them to Giselle, and she said that I had missed the point. Yes, they had sexual fantasy, but that wasn't what they were about. At their core, they were stories of a man who wanted nothing more than to love a woman and have her return that love. I realized she was right and let her read them each time Beast completed a new one. Little did I know that she had decided a year ago to share the books with you. But, it seems it was for the best."

Beauty couldn't move, shocked that her friend Giselle had a sister who was a sorceress.

The woman began speaking again. "I have left the enchantment on the manor for the rest of this evening, but in the morning it will be gone, so get any provisions you need for the next few days. And Beauty, your father is awake now. You may want to use the mirror to talk to him and allay his concerns. Now, I am off. I need to deal with Mr. Dumas."

Then she vanished.

Beast stood and wrapped his arms around Beauty, and she tried to breathe evenly. It was over, all over. She felt warm in his arms, happy to be there. "Everything is going to be alright," Beast whispered in her ear. Only his voice was his new voice, his Emile voice. She supposed she should get used to calling him that.

"At least for us," she said, pulling away from him, and walking toward the stairs. She wanted to get to the mirror and see her father. "I wonder what she's going to do to Dumas."

A low, throaty growl escaped Beast. Beauty turned to see whether he still looked like a man. He did, but clearly he had retained some beastly attributes. "Whatever she does to him, he deserves worse."

They ascended the stairs and found the secret room. Beauty was able to use the mirror to see her father. She wasn't sure if the sorceress had cast some spell or not, but she was able to project and talk to Pierre. He told her his head hurt, but other than that he seemed well. Beauty said she and Emile would come tomorrow to see him. He seemed he'd be well enough overnight. With that, she ended the conversation, and the mirror returned to its normal reflective surface.

Beauty turned to find her new Beast staring at her with a familiar gleam in his eyes. "What?" she asked.

He gently touched her ear, sliding his fingers down her neck, gliding across her collarbone, down her bosom, where he rubbed his thumb in a circular motion on Beauty's right breast. She felt warm where he touched her. She looked up and smiled. "I think I know what's on your mind," she said.

"I just want to see if this body fits as well with yours as my other one did." He leaned forward and kissed her. "Would you like to see?"

"Yes, Beast," she said, sliding her hand up his shirt, feeling his stomach muscles and his muscular chest. It was different, but definitely worth exploring.

He lifted Beauty in his arms, and started toward her bedroom. "And definitely call me Beast tonight, because I am going to be one."

THE END

***Thank you for taking time to read *Beauty & Her Beastly Love*. If you enjoyed it, please consider telling your friends or posting a short review. Word of mouth is an author's best friend and much appreciated. Thank you.

Turn the page if you want to read the first chapter of the next book in this series: *Cinders & Ash: A Cinderella Story*. ***

CINDERS & ASH: A CINDERELLA STORY

1

Ella had delivered the sketches of plants to Mr. Halliwell, the owner of the apothecary that sat at the edge of the town market. She'd done this today, as discreetly as she had on any delivery day for the previous six months. He'd paid her a small sum, which she had tucked in her shoe, so her family wouldn't know about it. When she first started doing this, walking with the coin squeezed into her already tiny shoes had been hard. But Ella was used to it now. In fact, she enjoyed the discomfort just a bit. It was a reminder of her plan. That if she could just save enough money, she could get away from her evil stepmother and stepsisters.

"Ella," she heard a voice call out, and turned to see her friend Faye running toward her through the market. Faye was a stout, tough girl who'd had a life as full of tough breaks as Ella's. They'd become fast friends, confiding in each other the mutual miseries of life. While they shared misery, Ella did recognize that she had it better than Faye. Ella's father had been noble. Even though Ella was banished to the cold north tower to sleep and treated like a servant, the home she lived in was much nicer than any part of the meager dwelling Faye occupied. Like Ella, both of Faye's parents were dead. But unlike Ella, Faye had lived in a home for orphans and just recently moved into her own little room in a boarding house. Faye was a little older than Ella, but as resilient as the wind and willing to give anyone a chance, so long as they did right by her.

That was one of the reasons why Faye was Ella's best friend. Ella had had a tough time making friends. Her stepmother rarely let her hang about and chatter with friends, the way she let her own daughters. Ella's stepsisters had friends and attended the social events, so they might find a suitable husband while Ella was left to do household chores and errands. But Ella was not sad about that, for if the rest of the girls were as vapid as her stepsister Bathilda, she was glad not to participate. And if her stepmother had been nicer, Ella might not have become friends with Faye, whose life was also mainly work.

Ella smiled and started toward Faye. She knew talking to Faye would make her late and her stepmother would be mad, but she wasn't going to let that stop her. If Faye needed something from her, she would offer it. Faye was really Ella's only friend, and while her stepmother had taken so many things from Ella, she couldn't take away Faye. This friendship was the only part of her life that Lady Kenna could not control.

Ella stopped in front of Faye, in the midst of the crowded street. "Yes, Faye," Ella said, a smile on her pink lips, her cheeks a little flush from the heat of the late summer day. Faye shook her head, grabbed Ella by the arm, and pulled her away from the heat and pungent odor of the crowds. People generally made way for Faye, for while she was short, she was quite wide and had a face like a bulldog, one that seemed ready to bite if you crossed her.

Faye tugged Ella into a little alley and then Ella knitted her brows and gave her friend an expectant look. "What is it?" she asked when Faye didn't answer quickly.

Faye stood on her tippy toes to look over Ella's shoulders. She apparently saw nothing to give her pause, but still spoke softly. "Ella, I think I know a way for you to save enough money to escape your family, like you want to. Save enough money in just a couple of weeks"

Ella was shocked. That much money. There was no way she could earn enough money in such a short period of time. Drawing the plants and earning money from Mr. Halliwell was a slow process. Her plans to start over in a kingdom far away required patience, and the ability to start over with the most meager of sums. She had been sure it would take more than a year to save up. "What do you mean?" Ella asked.

"There's a man, a man who is willing to pay girls for their time," she said, her voice low. "He'll pay them a whole king's gold for a night of work."

Ella narrowed her eyes and focused on Faye, trying to figure out the catch. There was definitely something wrong with that offer. That was a month of pay for a night of "work." She gritted herself and asked, "What kind of work?"

Faye lowered her eyes for a moment, then looked up at her friend. "The kind of thing your stepmother tried to get you to do with that gentleman a few months ago."

Ella balled her hands into fists and tried not to let the disappointment she felt turn into anger. She remembered the time her stepmother had told her a man was going to pay for the privilege of painting Ella. She'd been sent to Marigold's bedroom to pose, which should have tipped her off. Only she had been naive then. She didn't realize, until he was asking her to disrobe and planting kisses on her neck, what he really wanted, what her stepmother Lady Kenna had really given him permission to do. She'd screamed, kneeing the man right in his dangly thing, and run out.

She ran straight to Lady Kenna and said, "I am not a prostitute and you won't make me one. If you try again, I swear, the spirit of my dead father will haunt you for the rest of your life. For all the cruelty you commit to me now is within your rights. But what you just tried to do, is beyond your right and you will pay for all eternity if you ever try that again."

She'd tried to sound brave and fearless. She supposed she must have sounded so, because Lady Kenna did not bring another man around to "paint" or do anything else to Ella. The idea of having sex with a strange man who simply wanted a body, not caring if it were hers or someone else's, bothered her. She supposed she clung to the memories she had of her parents' marriage: happy, kind, loving, and filled with mutual adoration.

Ella shook her head. "I can't," she sputtered. "Faye, you know I can't do that."

Faye frowned. "It's a lot of money, Ella. It won't be so bad to do it. And you'd be able to get away from that torture Lady Kenna heaps on you each day."

Ella thought about her dream of walking out on that hag who had inherited all of her father's estate, who had spent all that should have been hers. Part of her hated Lady Kenna for her cruelty, but part of her understood it. It was nearly impossible for noble women to earn money of their own. At least noble women who wanted to pretend they had the wealth to accommodate their station. They were dependent on men for everything, so when Ella's father had died,

Lady Kenna had to make sure she was taken care of, that her daughters were taken care of. That, Ella understood. What she didn't understand was why Lady Kenna couldn't include her in the family, why Ella couldn't benefit from the largesse. She closed her eyes, breathed out. She'd had Lady Kenna as a stepmother and Marigold and Bathilda as stepsisters, for the last nine years and withstood it well enough.

A few months ago, Ella had gotten lucky by running into Mr. Halliwell in the woods near her home. She was drawing a bird on some scraps of paper she'd saved, when she spotted Mr. Halliwell stooped over collecting plants to use in his medicines. When he saw how well she'd drawn the bird, he asked if she could sketch some plants for him. He was training his sons to apprentice him, but knew that the oldest wanted the current business, while the youngest planned to open an apothecary in a town further over that had no such shop. He wanted to give the youngest information to take with him, but his arthritis had made it impossible for him to draw anything. Halliwell had agreed to pay her to draw some of the herbs he used, and then his son would write the pertinent information beneath it. Mr. Halliwell didn't pay a lot, but it was more than nothing, which is what Ella received from Lady Kenna. So, she'd happily taken the assignments. And if he kept giving them to her, she'd have enough money to leave. "I'm already halfway to my goal, Faye. Thank you, but I don't need this."

Faye frowned. "I thought at least one of us could get out," she said.

"Why don't you do it, Faye?" Ella asked encouragingly.

Faye shook her head, looked down at her feet. "You know why, Ella. I'm not pretty. Not like you. You've got the most gorgeous blonde hair ever, big bosoms, a nice figure. You'd be perfect for this. The man told me he needed a pretty girl. He laughed when I suggested me, but I told him I'd send my friend instead. And it's not like it would be riff-raff. Apparently, a cousin of the King or something is visiting and wants some companionship."

Ella stared at Faye. That was interesting. A royal relation who wanted a prostitute. "And where was I supposed to go?" she asked, more out of curiosity than any intention to go.

"He said to meet at the rear castle gate at 10 tonight, and to say that you were Faye's friend who wanted to inquire about royal nuts."

Ella couldn't help but laugh. That was the most ridiculous thing she'd ever heard. "Faye," she said. "Are you sure he wasn't foolin' on you?"

Faye shook her head. "No, he's a royal servant. I seen him before." She paused, then added, dreamily, "He wears such fine clothing. It always looks so soft and warm and clean. Not like the stuff we wear."

Ella nodded. She knew of such clothes. They were the kind that Lady Kenna, Bathilda and Marigold wore. Fine, expensive and not for her. She sighed and tilted her head skyward. It was a dark orangish purple. The sun was setting. She grabbed Faye, wrapping her arms as much around her stout friend as she could. "Thank you for thinking of me for this, but I can't. And I have to get home or Lady Kenna will have my hide."

Faye nodded. Ella pulled away and ran toward home. She had to hurry.

***If you enjoyed this preview, the rest of the story is available for purchase. For more details, go to <u>www.rosettabloom.com</u>. ***

Also by Rosetta Bloom

<u>The Princess, the Pea and the Night of Passion</u>. If you love royal romances, and princesses in distress, you'll love this story!

In this grown-up version of the famous fairy tale, Princess Adara is running from her old life and a forced betrothal. Adara wants love and passion, but knows she can't get them back home. When a raging storm halts her escape, Adara seeks refuge in the first dwelling she sees.

Prince Richard is tired of the trite, vain, frigid princesses his mother introduces him to in hopes he'll marry. On this stormy night, he's in the mood to love a woman, but he's all alone. Then, Adara arrives on the castle doorstep, saying she's a princess in need of help. The queen is doubtful and decides to lock Adara in a room with a pea to determine if the girl is a real princess. Richard believes the beautiful, charming stranger, but he wants her locked in a bedroom for other reasons.

When Richard and Adara hook up, there's more than a pea-sized bit of passion involved....

<u>Cinders & Ash: A Cinderella Story</u>. Ella would like nothing more than to leave her wicked stepmother and spoiled stepsisters behind. Only, she needs money to do so. The young lass has been secretly working for a local shopkeeper to earn some cash, but when her stepmother, Lady Kenna, finds out, she gets her stepdaughter fired, and takes all the cash. Ella's friend suggest she head to the castle for a job that pays well and requires not a ton of effort. Desperate to get away, Ella consents.

Ash is a prince confined to a castle. The queen is convinced magic fairies are real and are out to do her son harm. That doesn't stop the young prince from having companionship delivered. When a beautiful maiden is brought to him one evening, he's completely intrigued. By her beauty, by her demeanor, by the fact that she'll only give her name as Cinders.

In this steamy retelling of the Cinderella story, *Cinders & Ash* find love, romance and a fairy tale happy ending.

The book is available in ebook and paperback form. For more information, go to www.rosettabloom.com.

Romance: Trysts Short Story Series
For details on this series, go to www.rosettabloom.com

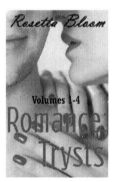

No. 1. Dr. Carter & Mrs. Sinn. Mrs. Sinn has been having heart palpitations and is in need of advice, so she seeks out the muscular, handsome Dr. Carter. The very forward Mrs. Sinn implores the good doctor to figure out the cause of her problems.

Initially nervous that he might be crossing the line, the doctor eventually warms up to Mrs. Sinn and takes an unorthodox approach to diagnosing his patient.

This story sizzles as doctor and patient heat up the exam table. FREE online.

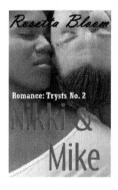

No. 2. Nikki & Mike. Nikki is a good girl who tries to follow the straight and narrow path.

When a breakup turns her life haywire, Nikki realizes it isn't enough just to be good. She needs to be good to herself.

Enter Mike, a handsome stranger with farm boy charms and a rocking body. Can he give Nikki what she's been missing recently?

In this hot and steamy tale, Mike and Nikki find each other and a little something else, too.

Romance: Trysts No. 3

No. 3. Tristan & Blair. Can a person know when they first meet someone that it's love? Can they know they're destined to be together?

Tristan met a girl when he was just a boy — a girl who changed everything about him. He knew she was the one, but she disappeared from his life.

When Tristan, now a painter, meets a girl from his past, he feels an instant connection to the sexy redhead. She's not quite who he imagined, but that doesn't mean he won't take this second chance to make this girl his.

Do second chances at first love really exist? Tristan gets a lesson in life's quirks in this red-hot, sexy tale.

Romance: Trysts No. 4

No. 4. Jack & Brenda. Jack is a firefighter, who's a man down at his station due to a massive snow storm. Alone, pondering the evening when he hears a knock on the fire house door.

Brenda is a nurse trying to get to her shift whose car goes kaput outside the fire station.

Jack offers to warm Brenda up and things smoke for the firefighter who has a thing for pretty feet and the nurse who's in need of some TLC.

ABOUT THE AUTHOR

Rosetta Bloom loves a good love story. She also likes a steamy tale with two characters who find solace in each other's arms. So, she writes romance and erotic romances, and all of them end happily, because Rosetta hates sad endings. If you want a story that has a few surprises, and lots of heart, then she's writing the story for you.

Rosetta Bloom's first novella, *The Princess, the Pea and the Night of Passion* was published in December 2014. Her second novella in the Passion-Filled Fairy Tales series, *Beauty and Her Beastly Love*, was published in January 2015. In May 2015, she began publishing a series of short tales as part of her *Romance: Trysts* series. The trysts are fairly erotic in nature, and lots of fun. They're called *Romance: Trysts* because despite their shortness, there's a touch of romance in each that should you make smile (after you catch your breath from the steamy love scenes).

More books in each series will be published throughout 2015. To learn more about Rosetta Bloom or either series, visit her website, http://rosettabloom.com.